MOMENTS IN TIME

A NOVEL

STUART FABE

For more information about this title or to order books, contact the publisher:
Stuart A. Fabe
Greencastle, Indiana
stuartfabe@gmail.com

ISBN: 979-8-234-04785-4

Printed in the United States
Photos Courtesy of Stuartfabecameras.com

Dedicated To

Louis Jacques Mande Daguerre
Who Changed the Visual World Forever

And

In Loving Memory Of
My Father
Robert Fabe
Who Taught Me How To See

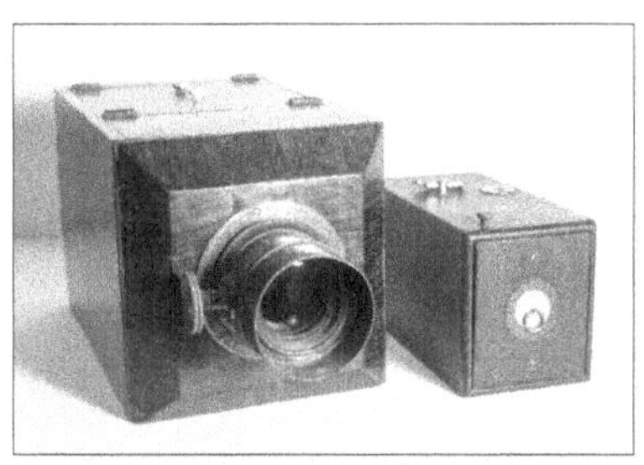

Author's Note

NEVER SET OUT TO BECOME AN EXPERT on the history of photography—nor do I claim to be one today. That distinction belongs to passionate collectors and scholars who devote themselves to the nuances of early photographic processes and how they transformed the way we see the world. What I *have* had, for more than fifty years, is an enduring fascination with early cameras—the elegance of their designs, the precision of their mechanics, and the powerful stories they helped capture.

Likewise, I never intended to assemble a comprehensive collection of antique cameras. Yet, over the years, it happened—first gradually, then with a joyful surge of acquisitions more recently. The reflections that follow offer a glimpse into the early history of photography, viewed through the lens of my own collection. This is not an exhaustive study but a personal one—an invitation to see how I've approached building a collection of historic and rare cameras that celebrate the beauty, innovation, and narrative power of these remarkable instruments.

So, where to begin? More than fifty years ago, shortly after graduating from the University of Cincinnati, I found myself searching for a creative outlet. Coming from a family steeped in the arts, I wanted to find a medium that allowed me to express both artistic and scientific sensibilities. Around that time, I read Robert Pirsig's *Zen and the Art of Motorcycle Maintenance*, which explores the balance between our artistic and rational sides—left brain and right brain, if you will.

My father was a college professor and a highly regarded painter, a talent I admired but did not share. Rather than follow in his well-established footsteps, I sought a different path. Photography soon revealed itself as the perfect synthesis of art and science. I devoured every photography book I could find at the public library, immersing myself in the work of pioneers like Louis Daguerre and Fox Talbot, and masters such as Mathew Brady, Timothy O'Sullivan, Gertrude Käsebier, Julia Cameron, Alfred Stieglitz, Edward Steichen, Edward Curtis, Dorothea Lange, Yousuf Karsh, Jacob Riis, and of course, Ansel Adams. Their diverse visions changed the way I saw the world.

Soon after, I built a darkroom in my basement and tried to follow in their footsteps. Every Saturday morning, while listening to *Car Talk* on National Public Radio, I experimented in the darkroom, coaxing black-and-white prints out of trays of Dektol developer.

Even as a young man, I was drawn to antiques. When I first discovered the sheer beauty of early wooden and brass cameras, I became captivated by the work of makers like Anthony, Blair, Scovill, Lancaster, Rochester Optical Company, and Kodak. Around that time—the early 1970s—camera shows were springing up in midwestern cities like Cincinnati, Columbus, and Indianapolis. Armed with my well-thumbed copy of McKeown's Price

Guide, I set out to explore. I didn't have much money, nor did I know exactly what to collect. My approach was broad and unsystematic, driven more by wonder than by wisdom. But everything about it felt magical. I bought what I could afford and learned all I could about the cameras and ephemera I encountered.

Now, sitting in my home office, surrounded by fifty or so cameras, I have the benefit of perspective. I've learned that you can't own everything—nor would I want to. My goal has never been to accumulate indiscriminately, but to curate thoughtfully—a kind of "survey," if you will, of the first sixty years of photographic history as told through the camera.

When creating my antique camera website (*stuartfabecameras.com*) and my PowerPoint presentation, it seemed fitting to start with pre-photographic devices and images. Before Daguerre's 1839 announcement, the only way to capture a likeness or a scene was through the hand of an artist. So I begin with a painted portrait miniature, followed by a Zograscope, a Scioptric Ball, a Polyorama Panoptique, a brass Schoenner magic lantern, and a few camera obscuras. If someone had told me years ago that I would one day own a Daguerreotype camera, I would've laughed at the notion. Yet today, I'm fortunate to own an early American quarter-plate chamfered box camera with its period tripod, a French quarter-plate Daguerreotype camera, and a half-plate Lewis Daguerreotype camera. To honor the Daguerreian era, I've also collected several cased images, an iodine sensitizing box, a Plumbe plate vise, an Allyn buffing stick, a mercury fuming box, boxes of Daguerreotype plates, a Scovill head brace, and various plate holders. To say I'm proud of these pieces would be an understatement. My current goal is to deepen my understanding of the Daguerreian and wet plate periods—the photographers themselves, their techniques, and the tremendous effort it took to master such a challenging craft. One of the great joys of being a member of the Daguerreian Society is learning and sharing knowledge with others—many of whom have forgotten more about early photography than I will ever know.

As my understanding of early photography deepened, I came to appreciate Frederick Scott Archer's revolutionary wet plate process, which allowed photographers to produce multiple prints from glass negatives. Although one-of-a-kind images like ambrotypes and tintypes remained popular, the introduction of multi-lens cameras—pioneered by Disdéri—and the use of negatives transformed photography into a viable profession. Just as importantly, the cost of portraits dropped to the point where the average person could finally afford to be photographed. This "democratization" of imagery reshaped the visual world for millions.

Inspired by this transformation, I began collecting cameras that embodied this visual revolution—models by Bertsch, Dubroni, Dallmeyer, Rouch, Scovill, et al. My collection grew to include wet plate stereo cameras and a fascinating variety of multi-lens designs—four-tube, six-lens, nine-tube, twelve-tube, even fifteen-lens cameras. With these innovations came the explosion of carte-de-visites, cabinet cards, photo albums, and photographic jewelry. Wherever there was an opportunity to create visual memories—and make a living from them—photographers eagerly embraced it.

My goal has always been to tell that story through the ingenuity of the cameras themselves. And, for the first time, humanity could witness the stark realities of war, from the Crimean battlefields in the 1850s to the American Civil War, as well as the beauty of faraway lands—India, Africa, Asia, Europe—and the majestic landscapes of the American West.

As the saying goes, "time and tide wait for no man," and by the early 1880s, photography evolved beyond the messy alchemy of wet plates. I expanded my collection to include cameras representing the dry plate era—portrait, view, and street cameras, as well as the ever-intriguing "detective-style" cameras.

Then came film! Sheet film replaced glass plates, and newly developed shutters enabled faster exposures. Then, in 1888 a visionary named George Eastman introduced roll film with the Kodak camera and the "democratization" of photography entered an entirely new phase. As Eastman promised, "You press the button, we do the rest."

Of course, there are countless ways to build a photographic collection. Mine is simply one way of telling the story. Many collectors concentrate on early images themselves—and while I cherish my daguerreotypes, ambrotypes, tintypes, and gutta-percha cases—it is the elegance and mechanical artistry of the cameras that resonate most deeply with me. If I were to choose one word to describe both the spirit of those early practitioners and my own approach to collecting, it would be "curiosity." For without that magnificent human quality and Louis Daguerre's great discoveries, we might still be wearing animal skins, pointing and grunting at prehistoric cave paintings.

And, just as I never set out to become an expert on photo history, I never thought that I'd ever write a novel, let alone the eleven that I've written in the last dozen years. It's funny how things unfold when you live in the middle of "nowhere Indiana" and are allured by the enchanting songs of age-old sirens such as curiosity and creativity. Somehow I came under that spell and became a storyteller. The tale that follows is a blend of imagination and my experience with early photo history. How boring it could be to read yet another pedantic treatise on the evolution of the camera and pictures. And candidly, in my life I've gone to great lengths to be anything but "boring." So, I hope my readers will allow me the license to go off in a direction that is not meant to do anything but entertain. After all, it's what we storytellers are meant to do. I sincerely hope you enjoy my imaginative story word-crafted from moments in my time, and along the way, perhaps conjure up and embrace a few reflections of your own . . .

Stuart Fabe
Greencastle, Indiana

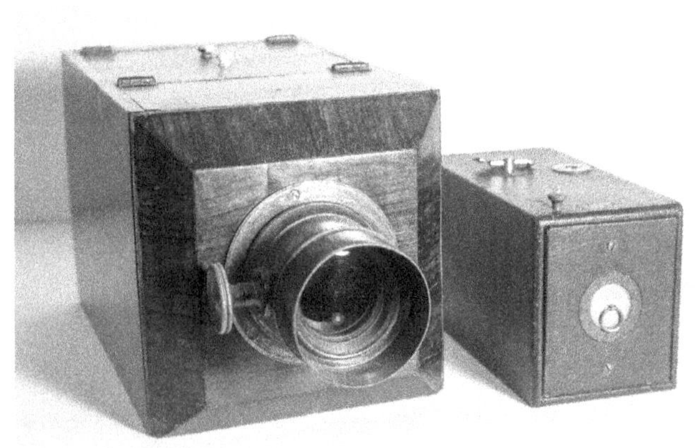

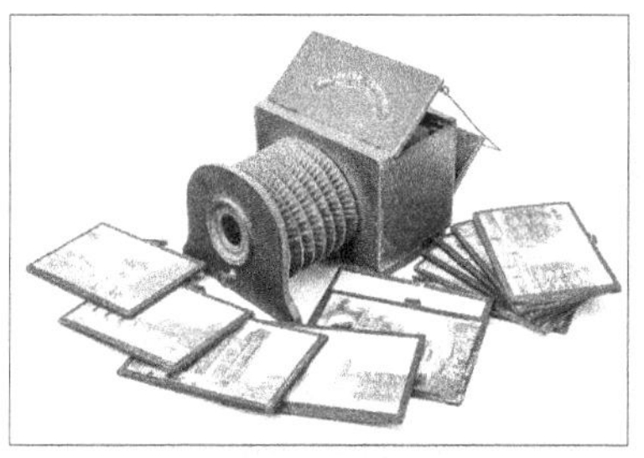

Chapter 1

Present Day
Along Big Walnut Creek
Near Greencastle, Indiana

AWAKE EARLY in my woodland cabin by Big Walnut Creek and peer around the still-dark interior of my cozy bedroom. I breathe in the moist air wafting off the creek some sixty feet away and know that soon the month of September will give way to fleeting, colorful leaves and hoar frost on the surfaces of my sylvan world. As I lie quietly, I notice light entering a knothole in an outside wall

1

casting an inverted image of a pine tree on the opposite bedroom wall.

"Ah, the camera obscura effect," I murmur to myself, recalling what I learned long ago about the nature of light in another time and place. I smile as the projected scene from outside brightly shimmers and sways. No sound, just a delightful light-born image greeting me as dawn continues to brighten into daylight stretching to the treetops, heralding the beginning of a new day.

"I wonder what today will bring, Kat Landrigan," I muse aloud as I pull the bedcovers off and set foot on the cool wooden planks. A moment later my frisky rabbit-friend, Clover, hops into the room, his curious eyes and twitching nose picking up scents of the outside world. "Yes, I wonder, indeed, Clover, but we sure can't find out lying around inside, now can we? And besides, we have to get ready for work. Why don't we take a brief walk along the creek before I have to leave for the office, okay?"

I pull out a tartan skirt and light-woolen top that I'll wear for work, but right now I slip into my skinny jeans, flannel shirt, and well-worn walking shoes for my brief jaunt outside. I light a fire in my woodstove and fill the coffeemaker with water and beans.

"C'mon, Clover, let's step lively now. We can't dawdle. Got a lot to do today to get ready for our next auction . . . you know, organizing, cataloging, and photographing the next lots for our early November sale. But first, let's see what the outside natural world has to offer us on this glorious morning!"

Clover is accustomed to our morning routine and bounds out the door onto the fieldstone pavers. The warm sunlight greets us both, and I throw a quick glance at the pine tree whose inverted, camera obscura visage I spotted on my back bedroom wall just a few minutes ago. "Good morning, Sir Tree, it's good to see you looking properly aligned instead of upside down and backward!" As if in reply, the tree's limbs and needles sway rhythmically, dropping a few pine cones and nuts as gifts along the path.

Clover hops beneath the tree and helps himself to a few tasty pine nuts lying on a soft layer of needles. Then, together we set off for the path along the creek's edge and a spirited way to launch our day. The soil underfoot is soft and loamy, making for very comfortable walking, and even though the sun has risen, Big Walnut Creek still holds foggy wisps in the shadowy areas near the first bend in the creek. We come to our customary stopping point by a large, flat rock and close our eyes, allowing our other senses to smell, hear, feel, even taste the welcoming energy of this hallowed ground. Clover leans his furry gray flank against my leg, and together we are transcended to other times and places, each with our own memories, each with our own histories. I reach down and lightly scratch behind Clover's ear. He purrs like a cat and leans even closer. "Do you ever think about the olden days, Clover, when we were much younger, and I was growing into my elfin ways? I am so lucky to have you as my spirit animal. You're such a treasured friend." Clover "purrs" even louder and burrows his head inside a pocket.

"Let's see if Miranda joins us today, Clover. Sometimes she does, sometimes she's off in her own world." A few moments later a blue heron is rousted from its perch and a lovely buff-colored doe steps out of the brush and stands on the path before them, her dark eyes sparkling and her white tail flickering in recognition and trust.

"Ah! There you are, sweet friend! Clover and I were hoping you'd join us this morning." Miranda snorts softly and walks to greet us by the big rock along the creek's edge. Together, the three of us close our eyes, and for a time, each of us is transported to private, personal places, worlds apart and yet co-joined through elfin magic.

Mindful moments pass and Miranda snuffles softly, giving brief playful nuzzles to Clover and a gentle headbutt to me before spinning around and disappearing into the safety of the verdant brush. "I love it when she does that, Clover. I love that we three are companions and can share our personal moments in time."

I look at my watch aware that my coffee is ready on the woodstove, but I'm not quite eager to return to the *world of now*. Instead, I choose to sit on the large, flat rock, with Clover by my side, watching Big Walnut Creek drift by, carrying flotsam along with my memories of times past, of people loved and lost, of dreams fulfilled . . . and unfulfilled. Clover and I make eye contact, as we have for many years now, and he jumps onto my lap to reassure me that the way I spend my waking hours these days continues to have meaning.

"I guess I'm ready if you are, my friend," I softly say, but instead of immediately rising, I lean back on the smooth stone, glancing upward through the trees, seeing faces and shapes in the clouds, thinking of my youth centuries ago among my elf clan, understanding that my existence in the *here and now* has purpose, that I am the holder and purveyor of stories, and that my work at the venerable Wesley Auction House in downtown Greencastle goes far beyond the selling of attractive artifacts. It provides me with portals to the past.

Several minutes pass, and Clover leaps from my lap and stands on the path leading home. "I know, I know, it's time to go. Thanks for keeping me on task, Clover. I know ... I have obligations to keep ... and much work to do before I sleep." I rise and the two of us amble, side by side, back to my cabin, back to my waiting cup of coffee, and a full work day ahead, clad in a bright tartan skirt and a light-woolen top.

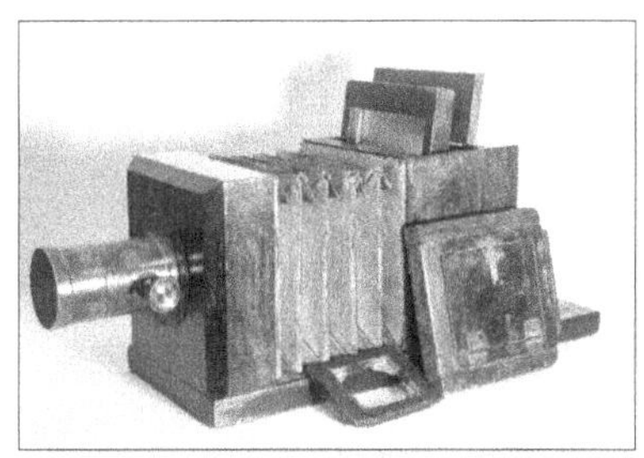

Chapter 2

As usual, the seven-mile drive into Greencastle is easy since there's never much traffic, even during rush hour, and there are only a few stop signs between my home and my office on the courthouse square.

"Good morning, Miriam, how was your weekend?" I ask as I enter Wesley Auction's lobby. "Did you get to spend quality time with your grandchildren?"

"My weekend was too short! Thanks for asking, Kat. Yes, the grandkids were great, but I gotta tell ya this old lady can't keep up with them. I'm exhausted! After trying to do fun things, make snacks, and clean up after them, I feel like coming to work is a vacation."

"Oh, but you're so good at it, Miriam, and apparently nobody broke a family heirloom or lost an eye, so it sounds like a pretty successful adventure with the kiddos." We both roll our eyes and smile warmly at the truth. "Are Kaylan and Emily in yet? We've got a full schedule staring at us getting ready for the November auction."

"Yes, they both got in early knowing that you're not going to feel fully relaxed until all of the early American ephemera and photography is prepared for the auction. You'll find them in the wareroom, probably elbow-deep in old Civil War photographs, flags, historic documents, and some pretty unique antique cameras."

"Excellent, I better go join them. Any messages for me? You know, where I live the internet service can get a bit wonky at times, so I sometimes fret that I'm gonna miss a client's message or something important from the Chicago office."

"No, I think you're pretty much up-to-date on everything, except for that wareroom full of 'stuff.'

But wait, come to think of it, we did get a strange voice message, left after hours on Friday. Sorry, I initially forgot about it because of my brain-drain over the weekend with the kids."

"Oh, define strange, and was it directed to me or another member of our staff?"

"No, that's why I say it was strange. It wasn't directed to any of us in particular, but my reaction was that it was from someone who seems to know us. Hard to describe, just a feeling I have. Actually, I saved it for you though. And, the caller's voice, well, it was pretty creepy. He sounded intelligent enough, but then there was his haughty laughter and labored breathing, followed by what sounded like a nasty threat. I pictured him to look like one of those demonic clowns from a Stephen King novel or something. Here, I'll forward it to you."

"Thanks, Miriam, I think! I'll be in my office listening to it, and then I'll be in the wareroom most of the day with Kaylan and Emily, joining them in the throes of curating nineteenth-century 'stuff', as you like to say."

I leave Miriam in the lobby and walk down the hall toward my office. Along the way, I take a few moments to look at some of the fantastic art and artifacts on the walls and in glass cases that are either part of Wesley's permanent collection, or pieces that have been consigned by collectors for one of our upcoming auctions. I see wonderful Impressionist paintings, a Rodin sculpture, several art nouveau pieces of glass, including a gorgeous Tiffany lamp, and works by Emile Galle and Alphonse Mucha.

I close my eyes as I stand in front of a stunning Mucha art print of a beautiful woman, with magnificent flowing auburn hair. "It's great to see you again, old friend," I whisper to myself. "I remember the times we shared coffee together at that small cafe along the Left Bank in Paris so many years ago now. I remember how excited you were privately sharing stories of your new beau and how much in love you were." I sigh with gratitude for having such a dear friend as Genevieve, and sigh again in sadness knowing that my magical, multi-generational existence as an elfin maiden means that I have outlived virtually everyone who was ever meaningful to me. I touch the print gently, whisper a few private words to Genevieve and move on down the hall.

As I approach the open doorway to the ware-room, I hear the distinct sounds of Kaylan and Emily's voices. I wait a few moments before entering to listen to their animated banter. As I walk into the room, I see Kaylan, who's seven-months pregnant wearing a huge African Nimba mask. Emily is howling in delight as her colleague struggles to get the heavy wooden mask off her head and shoulders. "Give me a hand, will ya, Em, I feel like I'm about to go into labor yanking on this thing!"

"Here, let me help you!" I announce, and Emily and I manage to liberate our friend and colleague from her predicament. "Oops!" Kaylan exhales. "Nothing like getting busted by the boss for messing around with valuable pieces of art."

"No harm, no foul, ladies, as long as nothing gets damaged, and we get everything photographed and catalogued for the auction in time."

"Gotcha, Kat! We think we're getting things pretty much in order, and thanks for not getting cross with us for trying to keep the mood light."

"I totally get it, but the Guinea people of West Africa might not look as favorably on people joking around with their important tribal artifacts. In fact,

I remember visiting the tribe a while back and see-ing them decapitate a European hunter for defiling lesser ritual objects."

"What do you mean ... *visiting*, Kat?! The tribe that made this mask vanished hundreds of years ago."

I've never told my fellow employees, or anyone for that matter, about being an elf, or the generations of people and places I've known over hundreds of years.

"Uh, right!" I manage to correct. "I mean from what I've studied this particular tribe didn't have a forgiving sense of humor when it came to outsiders making light of their heritage."

My two colleagues look at me skeptically, not knowing exactly where I'm coming from. "Well, I know you two have a lot to do, and I'll return shortly to help you out, but first I need to stop in my office to work on a few things."

I see that both of them still have befuddled expressions on their faces as I exit the wareroom. I walk further down the hallway, chiding myself to be more careful about what I say about my longevity.

Believe it or not, it isn't easy having magical powers or being hundreds of years old. Aside from a few other elves, everyone I've ever known is long gone, and even my closest associates wouldn't be able to view me the same way if they knew I had, uh, certain powers. "Gotta be much more careful!"

I reach my office door, enter, and turn on the light. I look around the space where I've spent countless hours working as a professional auctioneer. It's cozy and comfortable, and I've surrounded myself with intriguing objets d'art and personal mementos from friends and colleagues I've known for a very long time. My eyes fall on a photograph of me with a special friend who was actually quite more than a friend. He was the love of my life, and now he, too, has been gone for a very long time . . . gone but never forgotten. "I still love you, Henri."

I sit at my computer and look at my calendar and to-do list for upcoming appointments and projects I need to handle. I also see two voice messages flashing on my office phone. I open the first one and realize that it's the voice message that Miriam was referring to. Instantly, I understand why

Miriam described it as being "creepy." The caller doesn't identify himself, but I hear an odd, vague *swooshing* sound. When he finally does speak, it's the threatening tone of his voice that sends a shiver down my spine.

"So, you people think you're so smart," the voice icily chides. "You think you're experts on antiquated things, and you profess to know the history and value of antiques and art. You pass yourselves off as authorities and make a living sounding like you know everything about everything and manage to profit by selling historic things. Perhaps it's time you learned how vulnerable you are and how little you really know!" Then, there's that swooshing sound again, followed by the haunting sound of haughty laughter before the line goes dead.

I sit stone-faced staring at the phone. "What the hell is this all about?!" I stammer aloud. "Why would anyone leave a message like that, and what does it mean that we're about to learn something?" After I calm myself, I call Miriam and ask her to contact the police. Our company has far too many valuable items in our possession to be casual about our security. "Welcome to Monday morning at the

Wesley Auction House," I say aloud to myself and then open the next voice message, hoping that it doesn't come remotely close to the creepiness of the last one.

"Hello, Kat, this is Nathan Andrews calling. I think you may remember me from some antique photography conferences that we've attended, here in Greencastle and Indianapolis, as well as the through the Daguerreian Society. You may recall that I've built a fairly important collection of rare and valuable antique cameras, and I think I could benefit from your guidance regarding the future disposition of my collection. So, I'm hoping that we could arrange a time for you to drop by my home and take a look at what I've got. Frankly, it's time for me to begin thinking about selling some pieces, and I think that you and Wesley Auction House are a very good place to start. When you get this message, I'd appreciate you giving me a call back at this number to see when we might be able to meet. I look forward to hearing from you. Again, this is Nathan Andrews. Many thanks!"

"Hmmm, interesting." I definitely recall Mr. Andrews and also seeing images of extremely rare and early cameras on his website. Just in case, I jot down his phone number so I remember to call him back after helping Kaylan and Emily in the wareroom.

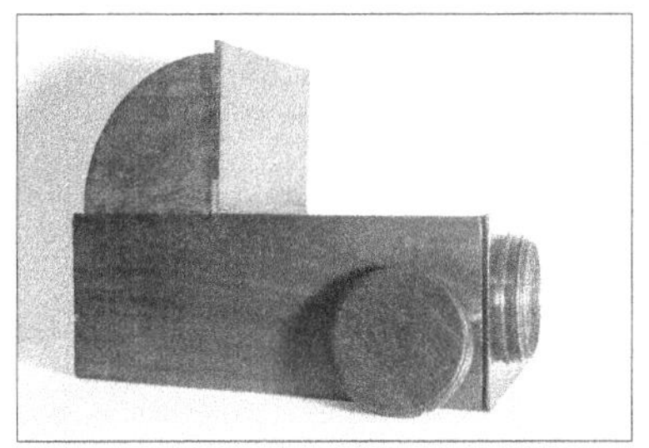

Chapter 3

My name is Nathan Andrews, and after seventy-some years on planet Earth, I've experienced a few different lives: I've worked, wandered, created art, written novels, loved people, messed up, tried again—sometimes gracefully, sometimes not. Now, I sit here in my home office, surrounded by my books, photographs, and all the quiet that comes with getting older, and I find myself thinking back, not with heavy regret, but with a kind of clear-eyed honesty. I can see the times

I lived up to who I wanted to be—and the times I missed the mark.

My lovely wife, Marla, keeps me healthy and grounded. We play the card game Cribbage at least three times a day, everyday, and have for years. There are times when she goes on these days-long winning streaks that I regret ever teaching her the game. She is a very formidable opponent, we both love the game, especially the swearing and cheating part! But, I digress ...

Right now, she's off on another Caribbean adventure teaching yoga at a resort, with her two fun-loving sisters in tow. They love the time in the sun together, and I'm very happy that the three Stanley sisters can enjoy life as they do. Frankly, as time goes on, I feel like I've become a bit of a *Hobbit*, preferring the comforts of home and hearth, and the company of our pets.

I've come to think that reflecting on life is a lot like investing in the stock market. We're happy to tell stories about the high points, the wins, the lucky breaks, but the losses—well, those usually get tucked away. We protect our soft spots, but getting older has a way of cutting through the noise. The truth is, I hear the footsteps of time. They're not loud or frightening. Just steady, and they tell me it's time to reflect . . . and prepare.

If you walked into this room, you'd see pieces of the road I've traveled: my novels, built one thoughtful page at a time; photographs that hold moments; paintings and family keepsakes; and then—yes—the old cameras, about fifty of them from the nineteenth century. Beautiful old devices made of wood, brass, and glass. Objects from a time when capturing an appealing image required good subject matter, knowledge of photo chemistry, good lighting, and a bit of good fortune.

I know these things won't go with me when I leave this world. Unless I plan to go out like a pharaoh, buried with all my earthly treasures. Even the pharaohs, I suspect, didn't get to keep their stuff for eternity.

It's the camera collection I think about most these days. When I was young, I collected modest pieces—nothing super rare, just interesting, well-made antique cameras I could afford. Later, when I retired from my years of nonprofit fundraising in Cincinnati and moved to the country, I sold that first collection to help build our art studio. I figured that chapter in my life was over … but these beautiful objects had a way of calling me back.

So yes—I started collecting again, but this time it was different. I gave myself permission to spend serious dollars on cameras that always fascinated me, cameras that I'd only seen in books and museums. Honestly, I don't feel like I've just acquired "things". I'm not a hoarder. I've been committed to preserving items that are historically important, and with some patience, research, and by building relationships with like-minded collectors, I've acquired cameras with great provenance, pieces that matter historically, with stories behind them. Over time, the collection has become rather unique, featuring extremely rare Daguerreotype cameras, wet plates, stereo and multi-lens cameras, view cameras, detective-style cameras, and very early film cameras … and unlike some collectors who privately do hoard their treasures, I've shared mine on my website, through talks and PowerPoint presentations, and with fellow enthusiasts around the world. It's been a very rewarding experience.

And now, as I sit here among these beautiful instruments of *light and memory*, I don't feel the hubris of ownership so much as the responsibility of being their respectful "steward" for a while. Things move through our lives, and we move through theirs. The question isn't what we keep. It's what we share and pass on.

As I sit at my desk in my home office, I slowly swivel around looking at each camera, situated on shelves or on tables. My first reaction is: Jeez, I really need to dust these things ... someday ... and then I consider each camera on its merits: It's overall appearance and condition, who made it, its year of manufacture, its historical significance, and what attracted me to the camera in the first place. Along the way, I've collected pieces using three guidelines: Rarity, condition, and price.

As for rarity I've focused (no pun intended) on acquiring very early daguerreian cameras dating to within a few years of the dawn of photography, as well as wet plate cameras, stereo and multi-lens cameras, detective-style cameras, wooden view cameras, and very early Kodak film cameras. In general, the majority of my cameras date from the mid-1840s to about 1900 and were manufactured in America, England, France, and a few in Germany. Most of the bodies are made of walnut, mahogany, or cherry and have gorgeous bright, brass lenses and fittings. To me, they're like pieces of "art" that skillfully recorded people, places, and history.

As for condition, I've only collected cameras that were in extremely fine condition. I've passed on some rare cameras because their condition was poor. The last thing I want to do is buy an expensive camera and wince every time I look at it because the woodwork is badly scarred or the leather bellows are damaged, or pieces have been replaced or are missing. Plus, if and when I go to sell the camera, I believe that most knowledgeable collectors would pass on it because of its flaws. My mantra is to always buy quality!

As for price, well, that subject opens up a wide range of emotions. Essentially, if it's rare and the condition is really good, I'll pay the price, perhaps after a little animated negotiating. An art glass collector I knew years ago once said to me, "You soon forget what you paid for something." I don't necessarily agree with that notion because I keep good records, but on the other hand, unless the price is astronomical, I'm going to give myself permission to spring for it. I mean, I'm in my seventies, why the hell not?!

In recent months, and with another birthday approaching, I've recognized that it would be prudent to begin winnowing down the size of the collection. To that end, I've sold about twenty cameras on eBay, but my problem now is that all the other fifty or so that remain are very special, and it's not easy deciding what else I should, uh, *de-acquisition*. Perhaps a conversation with Kat Landrigan will provide some clarity, but ultimately, I'll have to make some tough decisions at some point. One of my strategies has been to post images and descriptions of cameras online, and to direct collectors to my website, so that my collection is well-known when it comes time to pull the trigger.

I gently lift my 1848 American Chamfered Box Daguerreotype camera from its wooden tripod and set it on my desk next to my original Kodak camera circa 1888. In some ways I view these two cameras as the alpha and the omega of my collection, with the Daguerreotype representing the earliest commercially practical photo process, and the Kodak being the first roll film camera. Trying to comprehend all of the different cameras and photo processes that occurred during that forty-year span is tough because the world went totally nuts for pictures, and major innovations occurred frequently. Each advancement in technology and photo-chemistry that came along gave millions of people the opportunity to own inexpensive portraits and see pictures of places that they'd only heard about. Isn't it curious how new technologies often have a way of further "democratizing" our culture?! I'll leave the pros and cons of new technologies to far brighter people than I am. I place the Daguerreotype camera and the Kodak back on their dusty perches as my eyes and mind wander over other "treasures" that I've acquired. Then, my phone rings.

"Hello, this is Nathan."

"Nathan, hello, this is Kat Landrigan from Wesley Auctions returning your call. How're you doing?"

"I'm doing very well, thank you, Kat. It's been a while since we've spoken. I trust you've been keeping busy."

"Yeah, very busy, especially preparing our major auction in November."

"Wow, sounds like a lot of interesting work. So, you obviously got my message. Do you think we can schedule some time for you to stop by my place and view my collection?"

"Of course we can, Nathan. I recall you previously mentioning that you own a very special camera collection, and after receiving your voice message, I went to your website and saw several intriguing examples. Definitely enough to get me excited." We chat a little more as we both check our schedules and agree that we'll meet at my home later that afternoon.

"Great, I've got directions to your house, and I'll see you soon."

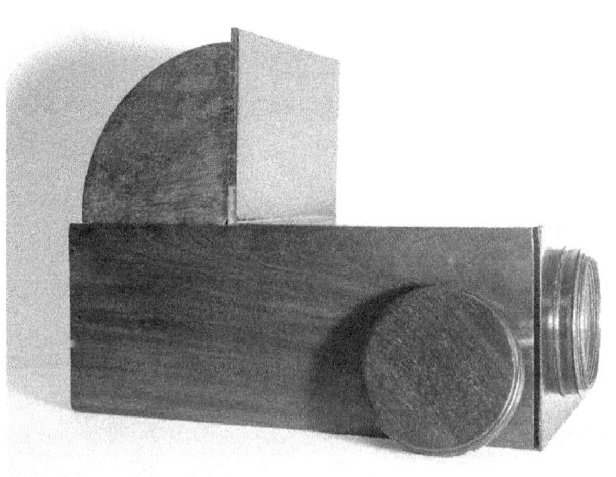

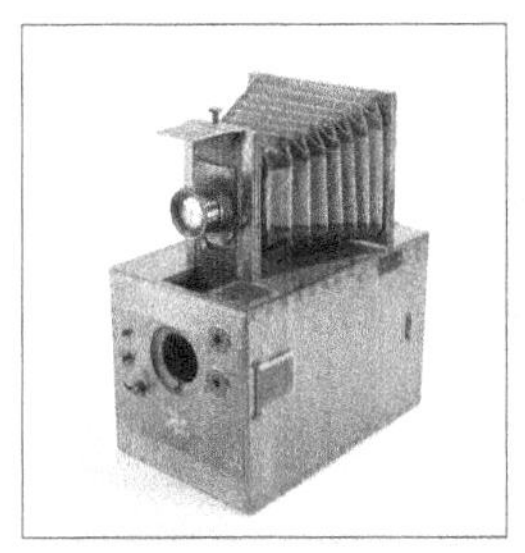

Chapter 4

After I hang up with Nathan, Miriam appears in my office doorway. "I called the police, and they're sending a detective out later today regarding that creepy phone message we received."

"Thanks, Miriam, that message is just so weird and more than a little unnerving. Hopefully, the cops can get to the bottom of it soon. I'll be spending most of today helping Kaylan and Emily in the wareroom. Please just let me know when the police officer arrives, okay?"

Meanwhile, some sixty miles away, a solitary figure enters the basement of the Indianapolis Visual History Museum and walks toward his office. The nameplate by his door reads, Dr. Mortimer Gleep, Curator, Photo History and Ephemera. He unlocks his door and lightly buffs his nameplate with his handkerchief, then enters his inner sanctum. He hangs his moth-eaten tweed jacket on a hook and stands in front of a mirror. His reflection startles even him. His scraggily white hair and unkempt white beard make him look far older than his fifty years, but it's his pale blue eyes, ashen complexion, and surly sneer that are the most unsettling. He takes a puff from his Albuterol inhaler and continues.

"Screw 'em all," Mortimer grumbles to himself, "And, especially those rich, patronizing collectors and dealers. Screw 'em all, I say. I've dwelled in professional anonymity in the bowels of this dusty, allergen-filled museum for far too long. It's time to, uh, make a statement." Then his sneer morphs into a haunting grin. "There's an auction and reception coming up, and I must make plans for it."

Some two hours later it's a welcome relief when the detective finally arrives at the auction house because my lower back's getting pretty tight after working through boxes of consignments in the wareroom with Kaylan and Emily. Plus, I can't get the tone of that caller's threatening message out of my mind. I asked my co-workers if they had any insight into who might make such a call, and neither of them could immediately identify a suspect.

"I mean, we all know that there are times when a consignor isn't happy with an auction result either because their prized item didn't sell or it sold for far less than they expected, but I just can't think of anyone who rises to this level of anger. I'm not sure what the police can figure out, maybe something through phone call records, but I'm pretty clueless at this point."

"We are, too, Kat! It goes beyond just being creepy because we're often here alone."

"Yeah, I get it. We do keep our doors locked, and we have security cameras installed in every room, but I hear you, ladies. Now, let's see if the cops have any insights."

I walk back to my office and see Miriam and a detective named Shane waiting for me. The three of us listen to the message again, and Miriam returns to her desk to make a copy of it for the officer.

"I just can't comprehend what sort of individual would harbor ill feeling toward collectors and art dealers. Makes no sense."

"I see your point, Ms. Landrigan, it definitely sounds like someone has a serious grudge against your firm. I'll see what our digital forensics people can determine when I return to the station. In the meantime, I suggest that you and the other employees keep your doors locked and your eyes open. I'll see what we can figure out from my end and get back to you as soon as I have something."

After the detective leaves, I quickly look at my calendar. "Oh darn, I almost forgot my appointment with Nathan Andrews today." I grab a quick lunch from my mini fridge, give some final instructions to Emily, Kaylan, and Miriam, and get myself over there.

My drive in the countryside heading toward Nathan's home provides me with a welcome break in my day. The sun is shining brightly with large billowing cumulus clouds looking like stout sailing ships navigating an azure blue sky. The autumn leaves have reached their full color and most of the corn and bean fields have been harvested. Large round bales of hay populate the fields, looking like chess pieces scattered along the landscape. Autumn in Putnam County is a delight to behold and very reminiscent of scenes I've witnessed over time in lands in Europe and the Americas. I see one field strewn with haystacks rather than the usual square or round bales, and it instantly propels my memory back to seeing a young French painter named Monet with his easel and paints capturing what he "sees" onto canvas.

Ah, those were the days when my *friend*, Henri, and I would tour the countryside in his carriage, stopping here and there, picnicking, drinking wine, and making love here and there. I sigh wistfully at the recollection, recover from my reverie, and then promptly turn left onto County Road 250 North.

Three minutes later I see Nathan's name on his mailbox by the road and turn right into his gravel driveway. For some reason, I instantly feel a sense of *connectedness.* Kinda like being connected to a supernatural Wi-Fi with energy streaming cohesively from all directions. I'm not exactly sure what it means, because I've not experienced anything quite like this before, but it feels reassuring rather than harmful. My elfin senses regard this place and time as where I'm spiritually meant to be.

I step outside of my car, and my feet seem to float above the gravel driveway. I'm concerned that Nathan is going to come outside right now to greet me, and I'm going to look like I'm in a wacko trance. Sure enough, I no more than finish that thought when I hear, "Hey, Kat, you made it!"

Fortunately my elfin logic allows me to keep my composure. "Hey, Nathan, great place you have out here. You and your wife must love the peace and quiet."

"Yeah, it's where we want to be, although Marla's away teaching yoga right now and returns in a couple of days. Before entering his home, though, the two of us stand quietly in the driveway eyeing each other.

Nathan's eyes take in Kat's shape and form. She's pretty and trim, but not slight, he observes. She appears strong and athletic. She has honey-colored shoulder length hair, untethered, and a broad cheerful smile, but it's her eyes where he notices something most unusual about her. They sparkle brightly in a youthful way, but he also senses something far deeper. They are eyes that seem to have experienced much, that have witnessed all the good, bad, and indifferent about humanity. It's surprising and confusing to him.

As I look at Nathan I initially assume that he just wants to form a solid impression of who I am since we really don't know each other very well, but I see that it goes deeper. As our eyes connect, I sense that each of us is *scanning* the other, forming opinions, showing curiosity, trying to *plumb* each other for trust. I sense that Nathan is an honest man, one who's figured out how to live life on his terms as much as possible. He's physically good looking in a senior-citizen-sort-of-way, and he appears to be bright and good-natured. I intuit that Marla is a lucky woman to live with such a fella. But, I digress.

"Well then, Kat, c'mon in, and we can begin my version of the *Magical Mystery Tour,* as John Lennon might've said."

I smile to my elfin-self thinking that Nathan doesn't have a clue about magic or mystery, and I hope to keep it that way. Strictly auction business!

We step inside his gentrified farmhouse, and I'm immediately greeted by artwork of various media. There's colorful art glass in the bay window, a woven Caucasian tapestry hanging on a wall, majestic photographs of the Milky Way over area landscapes, and a great blend of mid-century modern furniture and lighting.

"I like your decorating style, Nathan. We seem to share similar design interests."

"Thanks, Kat! Marla and I enjoy mixing things up." He smiles and confesses, "Most of the time we agree . . . but not always! Keeps things interesting!" We walk around his first floor more, and he proudly shows me some non-photographic pieces of art and sculpture they've collected over the years, some by great local artists such as Rees, Tweedie, and Reeves.

Nathan opens a door off the entry hall, and he shows me a major new wing on their home. "Since Marla and I prefer to 'age in place,' we recently completed this addition. The entire upstairs is now family and guest quarters, plus my office." We walk inside the new addition, and I'm excited to see more art adorning their sleeping quarters, plus their large tiled bathroom, huge walk-in closet, and laundry area.

"Looks to me like you two have done it right, Nathan!"

"We're pretty happy. We still want to do some fresh decorating though. Our home is always a work in progress. C'mon, let's head up to my office."

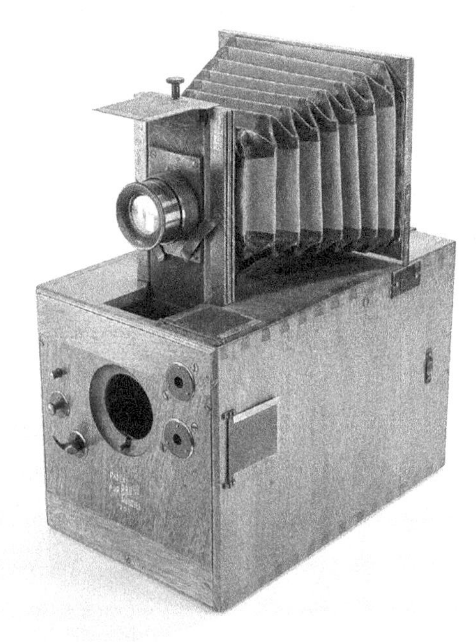

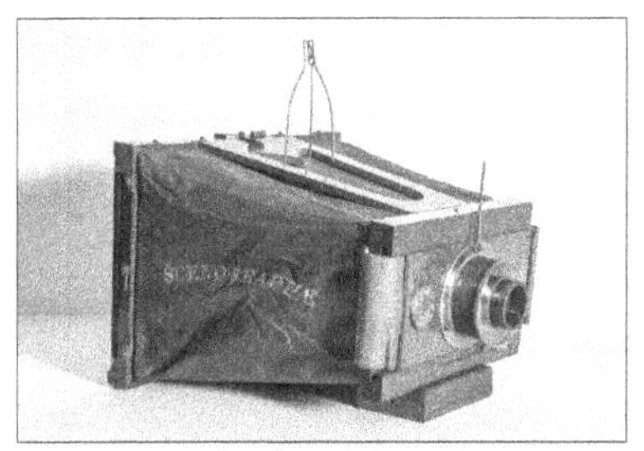

Chapter 5

THE MOMENT I STEP INSIDE Nathan's office, I feel the same sensation as I did on the driveway, as if my feet have lifted a few inches off the ground . . . *a lightness of being.* "Wow!" I say aloud.

"Kat, why don't you take a few minutes to privately look at the cameras. I sometimes find that when I bring someone up here, I immediately start talking, and I'd rather not distract you with my banter. I need to check on something downstairs, then I'll be right back."

"Thanks, Nathan, this is a lot to take in." Nathan leaves his office, and my eyes begin to do what they've always done when I'm first surveying a collection. I look for the most impressive pieces. And, I don't have to look far because sitting on a period wooden tripod I see a very rare American Chamfered Box Daguerreotype camera, circa 1848, standing next to a Lewis Daguerreotype half-plate camera, next to a stunning French Daguerreotype, each in immaculate original condition. From there, I look at cameras on shelves that I've only ever seen in books and museums, never in a private collection. There are very early wet plate cameras, stereo and multi-lens cameras, and concealed-cameras that a detective might've used. It's clear to me that Nathan Andrews is a very savvy collector, with a taste for authentic rarity reflecting the first several decades of photographic history.

Nathan returns. "This is quite impressive, Nathan, do you mind sharing some details about these? I have the time if you do."

"Of course, Kat, it's not every day that I get to talk about these cameras with a knowledgable professional."

"Well, thank you for that! No doubt, your vintage cameras provide stories that I'm eager to understand. There's something about them that calls to me." I look at Nathan and see that he's looking into my eyes, again, seeming to plumb my soul, searching for my sincerity about something so meaningful to him.

We spend the next hour getting further acquainted and talking about individual cameras and the kind of services that Wesley Auction House provides. Nathan finds that Kat represents her firm very well, offering clear, concise information about the auction process and how Wesley would promote any cameras he might be willing to consign for sale. I tell him about the upcoming auction of early American photography and ephemera in November, and mentally Nathan makes a note to decide which cameras he might be willing to part with. It's a tough decision, though, because he owns great pieces. Nathan and I talk more ...

"Here, Kat, check this out," as he hands her a stunning Scenographe camera made in France around 1879. It's a view camera whose bellows isn't the typical leather, but made of green silk with bright gold lettering. As I hold it, I instantly feel my body and mind change. I say nothing at first, just wanting to comprehend the mystical sensations I'm feeling. Then, I say, "It feels alive to me,"

"Hmm, that's great," Nathan laughs. "I get pretty excited myself."

"No, I'm serious, Nathan."

I close my eyes, and the Scenographe seems to transport me in time to when this camera was actively used in the 1880s. As if in a virtually real hologram, I visualize a lively Parisian street scene, with people on foot and in carriages. I even hear voices and laughter. It's fascinating in its realness. I'm not sure how much time has passed when I hear Nathan's voice. "Earth to Kat! Come in, Kat!" I hear his jocular words hanging in the air.

"Oh, sorry, Nathan, I seem to have gotten a bit caught up in this camera." Nathan looks at me curiously and then directs my attention to a shelf displaying other rarities such as a solid brass Bertsche wet plate camera, a Bruns detective camera, a Marion Academy, an original Kodak film camera, and a stunning Dallmeyer sliding-box stereo camera. And, unbeknown to Nathan, each time I touch one, I'm briefly transported back in time and get glimpses of the photographer, his subjects and their locations. I've never experienced anything like this before, and it's everything I can do to maintain my composure and carry on a reasonably intelligent conversation with Nathan.

"So, what do you think, Kat?"

"Honestly, Nathan, I'm not quite sure what to say other than you have truly put together a rather *magical* collection, and I would love having the opportunity to spend more time going over them with you again, if you're agreeable. We've auctioned many other nineteenth-century cameras and photographic ephemera in the past, but what you've collected here is truly unique. While many other collectors often collect things just because they can never have enough, it's obvious to me that you've wanted to own fewer pieces that display an early timeline of photo history. In truth, I'm not sure that you should auction any of them without considering their being purchased by a major museum for their permanent collection."

"Well, that's certainly encouraging news, Kat, and I must admit that my buttons are bursting with pride by your glowing words. I've definitely considered selling or perhaps even donating my collection to a major museum, but I struggle with that notion. I'm realistic enough to know that if I donated my collection to a museum, most of it would likely languish in some dark basement, rarely seeing the light of day again. Plus, the museum would probably want me to contribute a lot of money to preserve and curate it. But, the worst part for me is that anytime I've emailed who I thought was the appropriate museum curator, I've never even received the courtesy of a reply. So, my thought of *working* with a museum regarding my prized collection hasn't exactly been a pleasant thought. And, that leads me to why I contacted you and Wesley Auction House."

"I understand and agree, Nathan, there are some museum folks that aren't the best, uh, communicators, but there are some very knowledgable folks out there who actually have people skills, and if you ever want me to act on your behalf with a major institution, I'd be happy to do so. The curators at Indiana University's Eskenazi Museum and Lilly Library come to mind."

"I appreciate that, Kat, and that's something we can talk about further, but right now I'd like for you to get further acquainted with my collection and perhaps for us to select a few for your November auction. How's that sound?!"

"Sounds very reasonable to me."

"Great, and you're welcome to take your time checking out a few of my other *treasures*."

I look at my watch and see that've I've already spent nearly two hours here with Nathan, but given my virtual, mystical experience with the green silk Scenographe camera, I'm very curious how many of Nathan's other cameras can act as portals to a time when the camera was actually used. Even after centuries as an elf, I'm pleased to know that new and unexpected surprises can still occur, and I'm excited by what may come next.

I look at my watch again and say, "As much as I'd love to spend the rest of the afternoon learning about the, uh, unique characteristics of your cameras, I promised my staff I'd return to help prepare for the November auction." What I didn't tell him is that I want to see if Detective Shane has been able to learn anything further about that creepy telephone message. But more than that, I need to process what I experienced holding the Scenographe and the glimpses of a virtual reality by just merely touching a few others.

"Why don't we do this, Nathan. Let's schedule another time for me to come back, and in the interim perhaps you can think about a few cameras you may want to consign for our autumn auction. How's that sound?" We both look at our schedules and agree that I'll return tomorrow morning to continue our conversation. As we depart Nathan's office, I shoot a parting glance at the green silk Scenographe. It glows brightly as if thanking me in some magical way for recognizing its *virtues*.

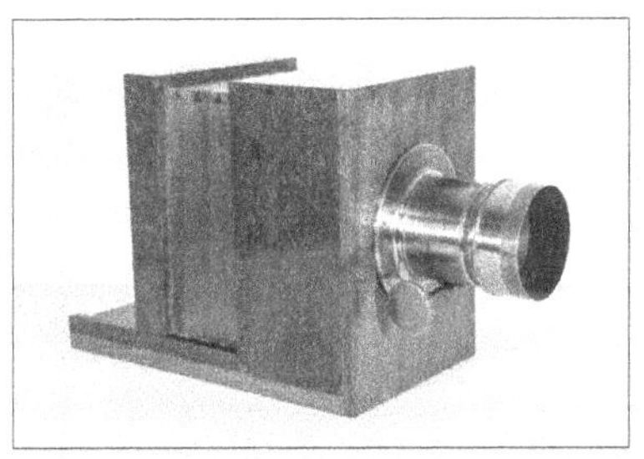

Chapter 6

THE DRIVE BACK TO MY OFFICE is filled with confusing thoughts. As beautiful as the autumn leaves are and as exciting as it is seeing farmers in their tractors and combines reaping the last crops from their fields, I can't get the thought of my experience with the Scenographe out of my mind.

My mind wanders ... How does something like that even happen, and why now? I mean, over the centuries I've experienced a lot of inexplicable stuff, but this virtual reality with another time in history is something I need to spend more time thinking about, and the hard part is that I have no one else I can discuss this with. I briefly think about fessing up to Nathan about who and what I am as an elf, but that opens up another can of worms entirely. Right now I think I need to try to figure things out on my own.

As I pull into my parking space at Wesley Auction, I see an unmarked car with a government license plate. Detective Shane, I presume. Hopefully, he's got something to share that his digital forensics people came up with. I walk in the door and see him looking all Columbo-like in his trench coat.

"Ah, there she is!" I hear Miriam chirp. "Wasn't exactly sure if you'd be back today, and the good detective just arrived a few minutes ago."

"Well, here I am! What's the good word, detective? Any insights into the phone message?"

"Well, we know that the message was made from Indiana, and we know that the caller didn't try to alter his voice in any way. From the sound of his voice, we think he may have a respiratory condition. He appears to be well-educated and probably in his midfifties. But, unfortunately that's about all we were able to deduce, so far anyway."

"Uh huh," I reply. "Not a lot to go on."

"Not so far, Ms. Landrigan, but we'll let you know if we come up with anything further. Obviously, I hope you'll contact me immediately if the caller contacts your office again."

"You can count on it, Detective Shane. In the meantime I don't mean to be rude, but I have a lot on my plate and need to get busy. Thanks for stopping by though."

It's frustrating not being able to get more information, and I'm not sure what I was expecting from a brief voice message. In reality, I think my frustration is more from trying to comprehend the *confusing* experience in Nathan's office rather than the detective's lack of helpful information. I know I need to control my emotions better in the future.

After the detective leaves, I walk back to my office and stare vacantly around the room, still lost in thought about the unexpected virtual experience in Nathan's office. I see all manner of photographs, printed literature and militaria dating to the American Civil War and know that I still need to help Kaylan and Emily in the wareroom. I sit at my desk, and my eyes fall on one picture in particular. It's of my beloved lover, Henri, and me together in Paris, and he's smiling at me. I pick up the framed photo and feel a surge of energy that I recall feeling when we were intimate. "Oh my!" I say aloud. "After all of these years, Henri, I still only have eyes for you!" I turn the picture around, and on the reverse I see words I don't ever recall seeing before. "Until we meet again, dear Kat." I feel a solitary tear roll down my cheek. "Yes, dear Henri, until we meet again . . . "

I hear a light rap on my door and see Miriam standing in the doorway. "Just wanted to make sure you're okay, Kat. You just seemed a little out of sorts with the detective."

I smile and reply, "Yeah, I guess I was, wasn't I? Sorry, Miriam, I'm just feeling a little stressed these days. I sure appreciate you checking on me though."

"Anything you want to talk about, Kat?"

"No, not really," but then I relent and tell her about the recent news I'd received from our corporate office in Chicago. "Actually, I do, Miriam. It appears that the suits in Chicago want to close down our Greencastle office. They think we're too small an operation in comparison with their headquarters and our bustling auction sites in Philadelphia, Boston, Palm Springs, Atlanta, Scottsdale, Miami, and New York."

"Yeah, I always suspected that might occur at some point, but I'd hoped to be able to retire from here. Any idea when this might occur, Kat?"

"No, not precisely, but I'm wondering if our November auction might be our last. I haven't shared any of this with Kaylan and Emily yet because I have very few details, but I know it'll be a devastating news for them. Let's please just keep this between us right now. I don't see any point in upsetting our co-workers until we know more. I'll let you know when I hear anything further, okay?" Miriam nods affirmatively.

After she leaves, I stare again at Henri's smiling portrait and sigh. "If only we'd been able to stay together, my love ... "

A few moments later, I get a message from Miriam stating that I have a call on line one. "The caller didn't identify himself. He just said he's an old colleague and asked to speak with you directly. My sense, Kat, is that it's the same person who left that earlier voice message for us. Mr. Creepy!"

I thank Miriam, but what I'm really thinking is: How does my day get any weirder? Right now all I want to do is head back home to my cozy cabin along Big Walnut Creek and hang out with Clover and Miranda. Then, I pick up the phone. "Hello, this is Kat Landrigan."

"My, my, my, if it's not the illustrious Kat Landrigan, world-famous auctioneer!"

I keep it professional. "Yes, this is Kat. With whom do I have the pleasure of speaking, sir, and how may I help you?"

There is silence at first, then a sound like labored breathing, followed by some odd, inhaling sound. "Sir, may I help you?" I repeat.

"I'm not sure, Ms. Landrigan. I understand from your Wesley website that you have an auction of American Historical Ephemera and Early Photography coming up in early November. I was wondering if you plan to have a preview of the consignments prior to the actual auction."

"Yes, we typically hold a reception at our office the day before the auction so interested bidders can see the lots in person. I'll be happy to add your name to the guest list if you wish to attend."

"Hmm, that sounds lovely, Ms. Landrigan, but I'm not sure if I'll be able to attend."

"Well, in that case, you can always register to bid online if you prefer. Your voice sounds vaguely familiar, sir, have we met before?"

"Yes, we have," the anonymous voice dryly replies. Then, I hear another huffing sound before the line goes dead. I stare at the phone for a moment and then call Miriam. "You were right about the caller. We should give Detective Shane another call. It doesn't seem like this guy is going away anytime soon."

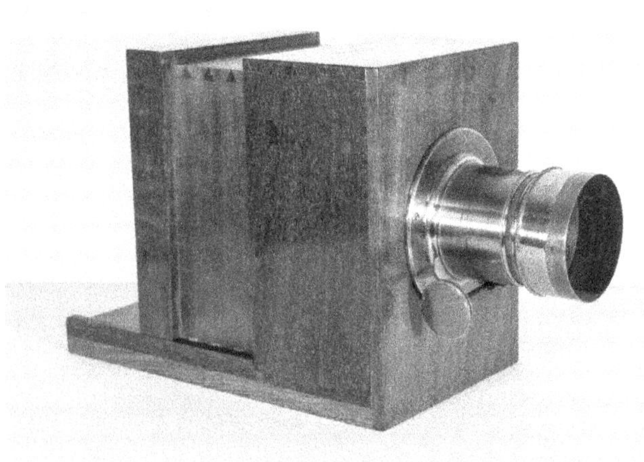

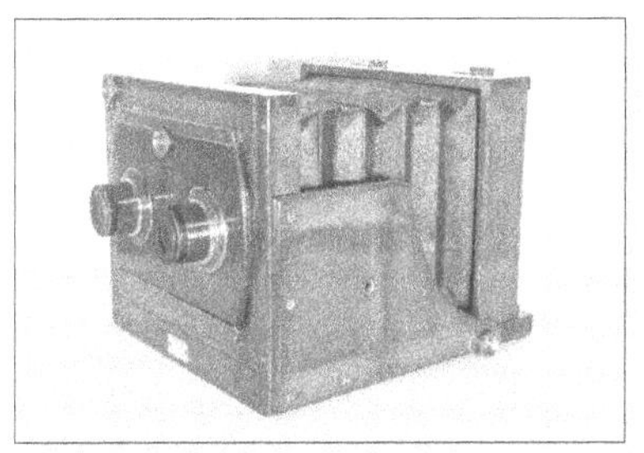

Chapter 7

THE NEXT MORNING I AWAKE EARLY in my cabin along Big Walnut Creek. I see the familiar beam of light streaming through the knothole in my siding and look for the inverted camera obscura effect of the pine tree onto the opposite wall. It's there, upside down and backward, shimmering and swaying, apparently from a gentle breeze outside. I then feel a furry bundle next to me and look down to see Clover snuggling along my side. I reach down and lightly scratch behind his long gray ears, and he burrows his head against me even more.

"Is it time to get up, Clover? It's so cozy here I don't want to move." Then, I recall that last phone call with Mr. Creepy and pull the covers over my head. "What next?" I murmur to myself. Clover thinks I'm playing a game of hide and seek with him and leaps on my tummy. "Ooof," I exhale. "I suppose it's time for our morning constitutional along the creek, huh?!"

Clover jumps off the bed and races around the cabin with energetic anticipation. "Okay, okay, I'm coming. Just give me a sec to put some clothes on and build a fire in the woodstove to heat some coffee." Five minutes later Clover and I are out the door standing next to the pine tree. He helps himself to a few pine nuts, and we set out along the path.

As much as I prefer to just enjoy the beautiful sunrise in my sylvan world, my mind forces me into the reality of preparing for our upcoming auction, plus the likelihood of Wesley Auction House being shuttered, and a very annoying caller. The only bright spot for me today is getting together again with Nathan Andrews to look at more of his wonderful cameras, but even that gives me a degree of anxiety, not knowing if I'll experience another, inexplicable portal to another time and place.

Clover and I arrive at our familiar large rock and settle there waiting for our dear-doe-friend, Miranda, to make a appearance. A moment later she emerges from a stand of mulberry bushes and strides gracefully to us.

"Well, there you are. Clover and I were hoping you'd join us." She briefly snuffles and nuzzles my neck, and I lie down across the broad limestone rock looking up through the trees. The sun streaks its golden rays through the limbs, and I think about the numerous paintings and photographs that I've handled over the years that represent light in similar ways. Art does imitate nature, after all.

And, I think about my life. I try to recall the faces of folks that I've known over the centuries. Some are vivid like Henri's, but others have been blurred by the vagaries of time. There is one thing I know for certain, though, and that is that I'm alone. Yes, I have a few friends and colleagues, but knowing that before too long, they too, will succumb to being memories. I love being an elf, but its ultimately a solitary life. I lie here with my two woodland friends, but otherwise I am alone with the perpetual beating of my heart.

After a time I softy say, "Okay, guys, it's time for this elf maiden to get up and face the day." Clover leaps to the ground, and Miranda stretches her nose down to nuzzle him. I smile at their warm communion and begin the brief walk back to the cabin, back to a fresh cup of coffee and a day of unknown possibilities.

After leaving a voice message for Miriam to let her know my schedule, I also call Nathan to confirm that we'll be meeting again this morning. An hour later I've fed Clover, showered, tidied up the cabin, and I'm on the road to his home. Happily, my drive through the country is carefree. Aside from a tractor, there's no traffic, and the only person I see is a protectively-clad dude tending his beehives. The name Sanders is printed on his mailbox, and I can't help but wonder how sweet his honey is and how many times he's been stung. I cross the little bridge over the shallow creek by his land and turn left on

County Road 250 North. Three minutes later I see Nathan's home and pull into his gravel driveway. It's a very charming looking place, and I smile thinking that he and Marla must be very happy here, away from the hustle and bustle of even a small town like Greencastle.

I set foot outside my car and immediately feel the same sensation of being levitated a few inches that I felt the first time I came here. Over time, I've given up trying to understand all of the vicissitudes of being an elf and just accept *what is.*

"Greetings and felicitations!" I hear Nathan call out from his back porch. "Ready for another adventure with my collection, Ms. Landrigan?!"

"Absolutely, Mr. Andrews! Nothing like immersing oneself in world-class antique cameras to start one's day!"

We enter his house, and again, I scan the interior spotting pieces of art I hadn't noticed before. Most notably are wonderful paintings by famed artist, Robert Fabe, who spent his entire career living, painting, and teaching in Cincinnati, Ohio, but whose art is in collections worldwide. "Very nice!" I say looking at a moody painting depicting a seascape from the Carolinas. Did you ever meet the artist?"

"Indeed, I did. Marla and I made more than one trip to his studio over the years. We found him to be a true renaissance man, and we love his work."

"We've auctioned several of his paintings at Wesley over the years. He certainly has quite a following given the number of bidders who participate and the fine prices his paintings fetch."

"That's very encouraging to know. We've collected his art because we love it, not as an investment, but it's good to know that there's a healthy market for his work. Let's grab a cup of coffee and head back upstairs to my inner sanctum."

As we enter Nathan's office, I once again feel the same *lightness of being* that I experienced in his driveway and the last time I was up here. "Prepare yourself, Kat," I murmur under my breath. "I think we're going to experience another, uh, unusual adventure."

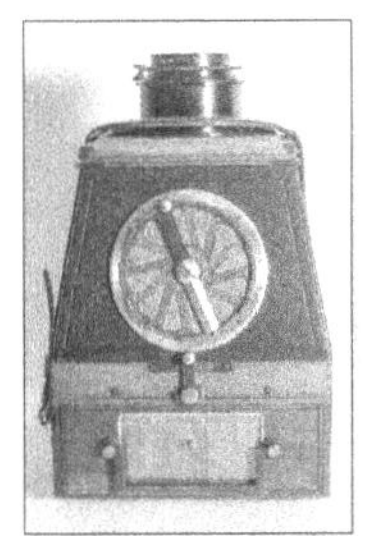

Chapter 8

"WELL, WHERE WOULD YOU LIKE TO BEGIN, Kat?"

"Okay, well, I see you have about fifty cameras here. Why don't you tell me how you chose to organize your collection and then select some of the really rare pieces for us to discuss?"

Nathan laughs. "It's not like I've had a master plan. I originally decided that I'd only buy a few exceedingly rare cameras, provided I could even find them. My thinking was that it was preferable to have only a few cameras knowing that at some point I'd have to sell or donate them, plus I felt it wouldn't be fair to Marla to have cameras staring at us from every corner of every room. I was very well-intentioned, but one by one that *plan* quickly fell apart, and you see where I am today."

"And, to answer your question a little more fully, I became enthralled with the very earliest of cameras, the Daguerreotypes, named after Frenchman, Louis Daguerre, who's credited with creating the very first commercially viable photo process in 1839. He changed the way we see the world! Years ago I never thought I'd own any, and now I have three, plus some very early Daguerreian images and processing equipment. From Daguerreotype cameras, I followed the historical timeline of photography and collected rare wet plate era cameras, then unique stereo and multi-lens cameras, beautiful wooden dry plate cameras, early detective-style and street cameras, and finally the earliest Kodak roll film cameras. That's probably more information than you were looking for, but that about sums up how the collection evolved. My main guidelines were that the cameras had to be rare and in excellent, original condition."

"At this point do you think your collecting days are over?"

"God, I sure hope so," I laugh, "but knowing me and my low impulse control, I'm sure I could be tempted by the right pieces. One thing that I've learned is that collections definitely have a life of their own."

Nathan's last words stop me in my tracks! "A life of their own?" I repeat.

"Yeah, I think so. Obviously, antique cameras are made of wood, metal, and glass which makes them pretty inanimate, but I can't help but believe that given their histories, and everything they've witnessed, both in front of and behind their lenses, that there's a certain *sentience* that we mere mortals don't quite understand."

I'm thunderstruck by his words, mainly because as an elf I purposely chose my profession as an auctioneer that enabled me to transcend time and place, to connect the past with the present. Now, I'm hearing this mere mortal claiming to understand the same sensibilities that guide my professional calling. "You honestly believe that?"

"Yes, I do."

I casually walk around Nathan's office, going shelf by shelf, display case by display case examining cameras I've either never heard of or only seen in books. "I'm very impressed, Nathan, and if and when you decide to sell your collection, we at Wesley Auction House would be extremely proud to offer these to the public. But, for now, why don't you show me a few of your favorites?"

"Thanks, Kat! Here take a close look at this beautiful French camera made by Jean Guido Sigriste in Paris around 1899. It's definitely a museum piece."

"Whoa, that is stunning, Nathan! What's the large dial in front for?"

"Oh, that's for setting the aperture and shutter speed. Supposedly, Monsieur Sigriste made it so the user could have hundreds of different exposure settings. I never understood why a photographer would ever need that many options, but it's a major feature that makes this camera so unique."

Nathan hands me the camera from a shelf, and immediately it serves as a portal to a time around the turn of the last century. I see, and feel, the bustle of a Parisian street scene that I immediately recognize. Surprisingly, the photographer is someone I also recognize, and when I look to my right, I see my old love, Henri, standing next to me. He's smiling and his eyes sparkle in the way I still remember. I nearly faint as I recall the day that Henri and I walked along this very boulevard and decided to have our picture taken. It's the same photo as the one in my office. I glance over to see if Nathan is aware of my *transportation*, and he appears oblivious.

A moment later, I reluctantly break free of my reverie and hand the Sigriste back to Nathan. "Mesmerizing!" is the only word I manage to say since I am totally stunned to my elfin core.

"But wait, there's more!" Nathan states as he guides me over to another shelf and then another, showing me gorgeous multi-lens cameras from America, England, and France that were capable of taking multiple pictures with just one exposure. Despite viewing all of these treasures in his office, my mind is still distracted by my virtual experience with Henri and the Sigriste camera. In order to try to regain total composure again, I guide our conversation back to business.

"Have you given any more thought about cameras you might like to add to our November auction?"

"I have, and I've identified five pieces that I'm willing to sell. They include three wooden stereo cameras and a couple of American view cameras, each dating to the 1880s–1890s. Admittedly, none are my rarest, but each one is beautiful, and I think this could be a good way to test the auction market. You can take them with you today if you'd like."

We chat a bit longer and then I look at my watch and say, "I could spend days looking at your collection, Nathan, but I need to get back to the office. May I reserve the privilege of returning again and spending more time witnessing, as you say, that *collections have a life of their own?*"

"Absolutely, dear lady. You're always welcome here." Nathan is happy to help securely wrap and box the cameras for his consignment with us, and we walk them out to my car.

"Our auction for Historical Americana and Early Photography is scheduled for November 7.

We'll have a reception the night before for consignors and prospective bidders, and I hope you and Marla will be able to attend. I'll send you the details, and of course, if you have any questions or concerns, I'm just a phone call away. Thank you, as always, Nathan."

We wave goodbye for now.

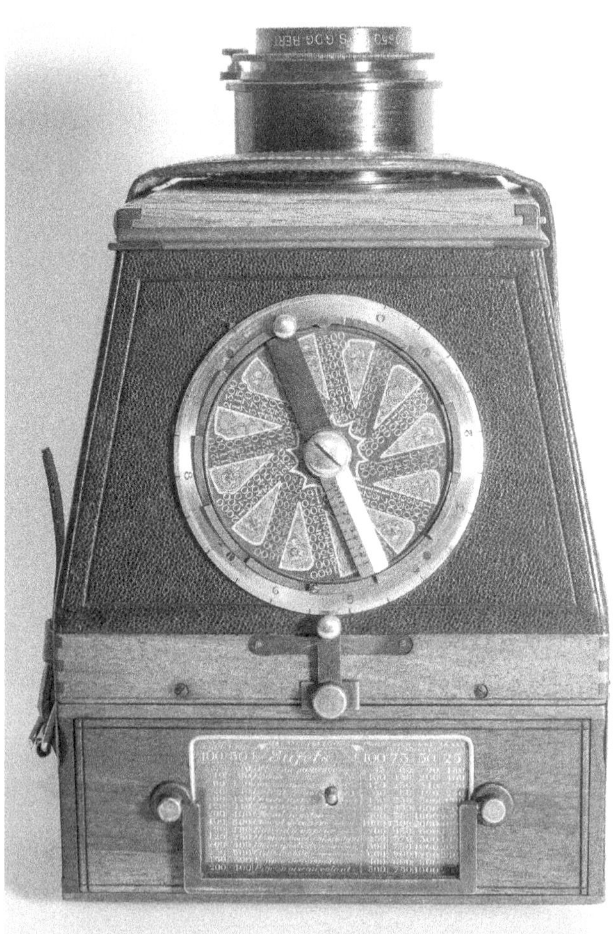

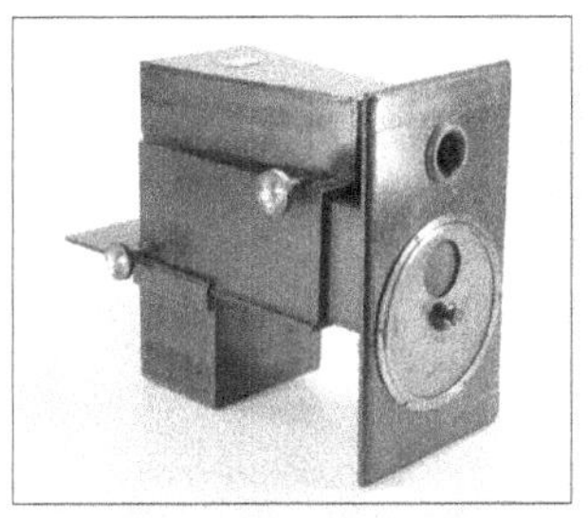

Chapter 9

THE DRIVE BACK TO MY OFFICE is filled with so many distracting thoughts that I'm fortunate there isn't more traffic. I pass over the small bridge along Dr. Sanders's property and see him now using his chainsaw to remove a fallen tree that is partially obstructing the road. I toot my horn and wave as I pass by, but he's focusing on the job at hand and doesn't respond. When I arrive at the office, Miriam is gone for the day, but Kaylan and Emily are still plugging away, photographing and cataloging final items for the auction.

"Wow, ladies, I'm impressed that you're still here. You're doing an amazing job! They see the cartload of Nathan's cameras I've wheeled into the wareroom, and both of them roll their eyes at the additional work I've just thrust on them.

"Gee, Kat! Emily and I were just complimenting ourselves for nearly completing this task. I guess there's just no rest for the wicked, huh, Em?!"

"Sorry, guys, I know you've worked super hard, but these are very rare cameras, and we're in business to make money for the firm after all."

"No problem, Kat," Emily replies cheerfully. "We *wicked* ladies are can-do girls!"

After a few minutes, I say goodbye to my co-workers and walk back to my office. It's quiet, and I choose to leave the lights low. I sit at my desk and just stare into space, alone again as I often am and have been for centuries. I smile thinking about my dear woodland friends, Clover and Miranda, and also about how much I've loved working with Miriam, Emily, and Kaylan. The thought of our corporate headquarters ceasing our operations is very sad, but I know that I've experienced much sadness over the years and have eventually recovered. I see the photo of Henri and me in the dim light and whisper to myself, "Life goes on."

My phone rings, but I choose not to answer it. I've had enough excitement for one day and figure that whoever's calling can wait for me to get back to them tomorrow. All I want to do now is drive home to my cozy cabin along Big Walnut Creek … to sleep and perchance to dream of former days.

From his musty office deep within the bowels of the Indianapolis Visual History Museum, Dr. Mortimer Gleep stares at his phone. "Well, I guess Ms. Fancy-Perfect Kat Landrigan is either gone for the day or simply doesn't want to take my call. No biggie! She and those other mercenaries at Wesley Auction House will soon hear from me again. I plan to attend that reception she talked about, and she has no idea about the, uh, *fireworks* that are coming their way." He takes a couple of puffs from his respiratory inhaler, leans back in his chair, and reminisces about the source of his professional angst which hangs on him like a funeral shroud.

"Dammit it all to hell. I spent thousands of dollars and years in school getting my PhD in Visual History, and all I have to show for it are some yellowing diplomas and a shit-paying job here at a museum that people rarely come to. Yeah, one could argue that I didn't have good counsel as a young student, or I don't have a winning personality as my faculty adviser told the doctoral committee, but that's all a load of hooey in my book. No, the real reason I'm languishing in professional and academic anonymity is because I don't bring in the big bucks. So yeah, if the truth be told, I'm royally pissed off because money-grubbing people that work for places like Wesley Auction rake in a bunch of dough dealing with snooty collectors. So, hell yeah, I'm royally hacked off and am directing my *pissiness* toward the likes of Kat and Company because they're close by and because, right or wrong, I felt that good ol' Kat snubbed my advances at the last Daguerreian Symposium. She probably doesn't even know that I exist. And, if that sounds petty, that's because it is, and I really don't give a crap! So, fireworks it shall be!"

After Kat leaves I walk back inside and am greeted by the silence I've grown accustomed to while Marla is away. It's not that I don't miss her while she's gone, but I enjoy being able to do, and eat, whatever I want. And, talk about eating, our two cats and little dog, Piper, make it abundantly clear that they're ready for a snack and some attention. I take care of them and then walk back upstairs to my office to work on another novel that I've been writing. After publishing ten adventure novels in ten years, I'm determined to make this one a little more autobiographical. Each time I've written a book, I wonder if it'll be the last one I ever write. Now, in my mid-seventies I have those thoughts again, and that's why I want this to be more personal rather than just another adventure story. I'm halfway through the story, and while it is more about me and my camera collection, I can't help but inject some adventure and magic into the story. I'm a storyteller, after all.

Our big cat, Jazz, jumps onto my lap while our other cat, Bella, takes up residence on my computer keyboard. "Hey guys," I admonish them. "You're *effing* with the creative process here!" It's clear that they really don't care about my creative process or my admonishment, so I gently move them out of the way. "Now, where was I?"

I look around at the cameras in my office and reflect on how much I've learned about the history of photography by collecting them, and how much pleasure they've brought me. The thought of selling even a few through Wesley's is a big step for me, but I have faith that the cameras I own are world-class, and that Kat will do her very best in presenting them to the public. Nonetheless, it's hard to let go.

I reach over and pick up the Sigriste camera that Kat held a few minutes ago and feel something I've never felt before. It's a surge of inexplicable energy accompanied by a momentary visual flash of a street scene that looks like late nineteenth-century Paris, and then it's gone. "That's weird," I say aloud. "Never felt anything like that before."

I then pick up the green silk Scenograph camera that Kat handled the first time she was here, and a similar sensation and vision course through my body and mind. "Whew! Maybe I need to cut back on the gummies." I look at the other cameras in my office, and one by one, I pick them up expecting to have similar experiences, but nothing unusual occurs. The more that I think about it, the more I wonder if Kat, herself, is the catalyst. "How is that even possible? There's no way . . . is there?!"

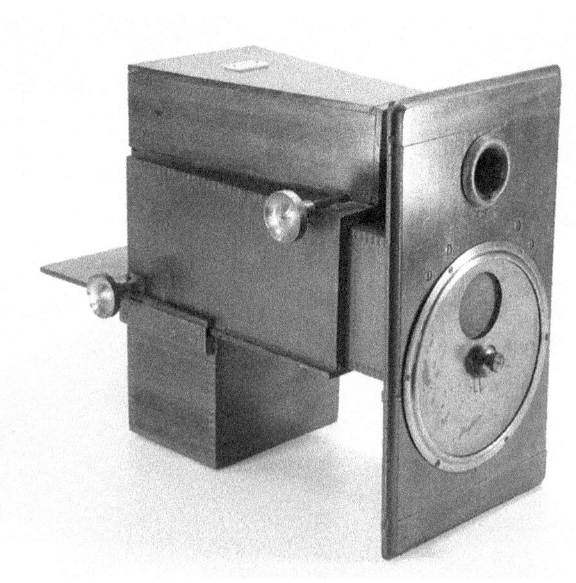

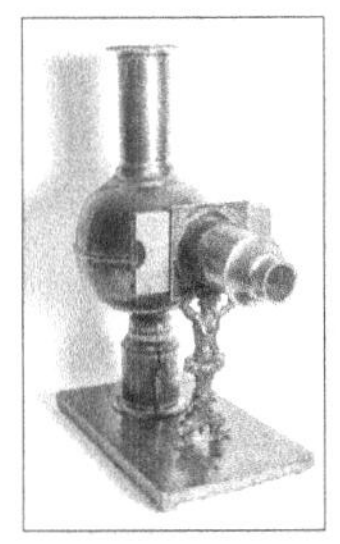

Chapter 10

HE DAYS GO BY and the colorful autumn leaves have given way to barren limbs and frost on the ground. It's the morning of preview reception, and the image of the pine tree that I've often seen reflected, upside down and backward on my cabin wall, is still there, but I know that with colder temperatures coming, I need to plug that knothole very soon to block the wintry air. So, the *camera obscura* image of the pine tree outside will cease to greet me and Clover each morning when we awake. As I've learned over time, everything and everyone eventually come and go. That is everyone except for me and a few of my elfin brethren who are scattered across the globe.

I quickly dress warmly and build a fire in the woodstove to heat the the room and the coffee pot. "C'mon, Clover, shall we head outside for our morning constitutional along the creek?" He's such a good-natured friend, but I can tell that he'd rather hang out by the woodstove. I reach down and gently pick him up and step outside onto the icy pavers.

"Whoa, it is a bit nippy today, my friend. Let's make this walk along the creek a little briefer than usual. Maybe we'll see Miranda this morning, but she's pretty smart and may just choose to stay hunkered down away from the wind." We set out together, and our sylvan world looks different without the leaves. Instead of broad leafy shadows, I see stick-like shadows from the barren limbs. It reminds me of the Robert Fabe paintings I saw at Nathan's house with gray, brooding skies and distinct branch-like shadows. We reach the large limestone rock where we usually stop, but it's too cold this morning to lie down on it. Instead, I watch the creek flow by carrying flotsam from upstream and think about my life.

Sadly, word has come down from our corporate office in Chicago that Wesley's Greencastle office will be closed soon after our auction tomorrow. It's, indeed, very sad because the Greencastle office was once a major, international auction house that eventually got acquired by Wesley. It's also very sad because Miriam, Kaylan, and Emily will lose their jobs. Only I will remain to organize and liquidate the inventory that's left in our wareroom. As I said, everything and everyone eventually come and go.

Clover and I wait to see if Miranda will grace us with her presence, but it's not meant to be on this frosty November morning. "C'mon Clover, I'll race you back to the cabin, and then I need to get ready for work." Clover is off in a flash, but I dawdle just a few moments longer to watch the Big Walnut Creek meander through the central Indiana countryside and think about times gone by and what the future may yet hold.

I arrive at our Wesley office around 9:00 AM and am greeted by silence. There are no phones ringing, no staff meetings or voices from clients or my co-workers, just art and artifacts everywhere bathed in stillness and quietude. I reflect on the many times I wished that things were quieter and calmer at work, but now I mourn the loss of activity and rue the *sounds of silence.* I enter my office and wonder when the ax will eventually fall on my position. Truth be told, I'm not enormously concerned about my livelihood because I've always been a survivor. It's my co-workers that I worry about the most. My phone rings, and I answer the call. It's Nathan wanting to know if there's anything he and Marla can do to assist with the upcoming reception. I think he's saddened about our Greencastle office closing almost as much as we are. He's such a dear fellow.

"It's great to hear from you, Nathan, and I really appreciate your offer, but I think I've got everything pretty much in hand. The caterers and the cellist all know what they need to do, and I've prepared my notes for brief introductory comments. We'll have a revolving projection of the auction catalog on large screens around the room, and we have all of the auction lots arranged on tables for our preview. Is there anything special I can do for you?"

"No, I just wanted to offer my assistance. I know this particular auction is an especially emotional event, and I didn't want you to feel totally alone."

My voice catches at his kind words. "I can't tell you how much that means to me, Nathan."

"Well then, we'll see you in a few hours. I'm sure everything will go great!"

After we hang up, I spend a couple of hours reviewing for the umpteenth time the myriad of details that come with staging a large preview reception. I look at the guest list again and see that we have a number of very highly regarded collectors who are planning to attend. Folks such as Pete and Barbara Schultz from Rhode Island, Michael Kramer from California, Rob Niederman from Minnesota, Rob Lisle from South Carolina, Katie Horstman from Ohio, and Wes Cowan from Michigan. These are true giants in the realm of early photographic history, people who've probably forgotten more about early cameras and images than I'll ever know.

Well, I guess I've done as much as I can for now. We'll just let nature take its course and keep our fingers crossed that Wesley Auction House's swan song is an event to be remembered!

I organize several scattered papers on my worktable, place a few files in drawers, turn off my desk lamp, and quietly sit in the dark to collect my thoughts for a few moments. Then, I look at my watch and realize I need to scoot home to get dressed for the reception.

The drive back is uneventful. There are still a few farmers in their tractors and combines cleaning up the last remnants of their harvest, but most of their work is completed. The view along Big Walnut Creek looks remarkably different now than it does during the verdant summer months. No matter the season, though, the creek always looks enchanting to me.

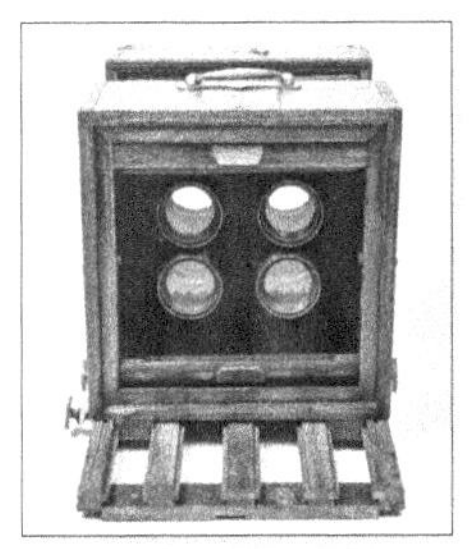

Chapter 11

W HEN I OPEN THE CABIN DOOR, Clover prances around expecting me to take him outside for another walk, but I bend down, lightly stroke his ears, and tell him that I need to get dressed for tonight's festivities. He's such a good-natured little guy, and he takes the disappointment in stride. I promise to make it up to him.

"What should I wear today?" I muse out loud. I look around my closet to select an outfit that is both very attractive and professional. I finally decide on going with a black ensemble featuring trim, tight-fitting slacks that usually attract some male attention, plus a form-fitting black cashmere turtleneck, and a trendy black jacket. For contrast, I choose my pointed leopard shoes and a lovely gold-and-diamond necklace. The diamonds sparkle brightly, and the gold color picks up the yellow hues of the leopard sling-backs and go very well with my outfit. As I pack the gold necklace for later, I have a vision of the man who gave it to me ... famous financier, Mayer Rothschild. It was about 1790, and he was an incredibly wealthy European banker who'd taken a shine to me which was flattering, but I knew that all he really wanted to do was get into this elf maiden's drillies which did not happen! I actually tried to politely decline his gift which unfortunately insulted him greatly because he wasn't accustomed to having his expensive gifts or his romantic advances declined. So, out of courtesy, I kept the necklace, which I love to this day, and I didn't have to surrender to Mayer's, uh, amorous intentions.

After making a light snack for Clover and me, I brush my teeth and take a final look in my tote bag to make sure I haven't forgotten anything. And then, I'm out the door heading for beautiful downtown Greencastle and a day that I pray goes without a hitch.

Meanwhile, some sixty miles away in Indianapolis, Dr. Mortimer Gleep arrives at his own office in the basement of the Visual History Museum. He sidles over to a mirror to inspect his visage. "Well, Mortie my boy, tonight's the night for a little pyrotechnics! In for a penny, in for a pound as the Brits like to say." He closely examines his long snow-white hair pulled back in a ponytail and his full unkempt beard. "Well, I'm certainly not getting any younger, am I, and what's with the ashen complexion and annoying skin tags?" But, more than anything it's the hollow stare coming from his pale blue eyes that catches him by surprise. "I used to be a nice-enough looking fella a long time ago. No wonder my boss has relegated me to the basement far away from the public. Hell, I'm beginning to even frighten myself." Then he flashes a menacing grin at the mirror and erupts with a haughty laugh. "Yessiree! Tonight's the night, and there's nothing those money-grubbing mercenaries at Wesley Auction House can do about it."

"Are you about ready, Marla? I'll go warm up the car."

"Now just cool your jets, Nathan, the reception doesn't even start for an hour, and there's no reason why we have to be the first guests there."

"But . . . " I start to say, even though I know she's right. "I'm just getting a little excited about seeing all of the auction lots on display, and I'm a little nervous about how my cameras will be received."

"Well, dear, just set your *little-excited* fanny down and play with the cat or something. I'm still about fifteen minutes away from being ready."

I do as she instructs, but our cat, Jazz, is more interested in chasing a fly in the window than spending quality time with his devoted male human.

About fifteen minutes later I hear Marla sashay into the room and ask, "So, how do I look?!"

"Wow, you look absolutely stunning!"

"You still know how to charm a girl, don't ya? Does this dress make me look fat?"

I realize I may not always be the sharpest pencil in the box, but I know there are only a few good answers for a loaded question like that. "You look absolutely ravishing, my dear. The dress is perfect. Have you lost a little weight? Your hair is gorgeous, and your jewelry goes with everything perfectly. In fact, you look like a young princess going to a cotillion."

"Really, Nathan?! I know that tonight is important to you, and I want to make you proud."

"Darlin', you're the prettiest girl on the planet, and you always make me proud. Now, can we please get in the car?!" She gives me a peck on the cheek, tells me not to muss her hair, and we exit our cozy farmhouse and climb into my Lexus.

We cross over the little bridge abutting Doc Sanders's property, and Marla tells me to slow down. As we approach his driveway, we see him and his lady friend, Kara, making out in his front yard. Marla reaches over, toots my horn, and hollers out, "Get a room!" They probably have no idea who we are, *and frankly Scarlett, I don't think they give a damn!*

We live only six miles from the courthouse square, and as we arrive, I notice that a good-sized crowd has already arrived.

"Oh, they have valet parking available, Nathan."

"Not for my brand new car, they don't! I'm not letting some pimply-faced juvenile delinquent drive my car. If you want me to drop you off, I will, but I'm parking this baby myself."

"Well, I'm not walking three blocks in these heels. Drop me off, and I'll meet you inside."

"Fine," I say. "Oh, and have I told you lately that you're the prettiest girl on the planet?!"

She gives me another peck on the cheek, and says, "Yes, and I love you for it! See you inside."

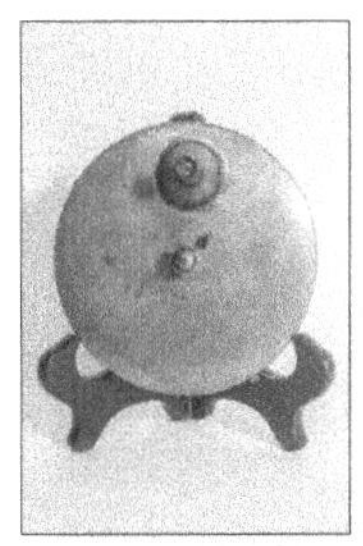

Chapter 12

AFTER PARKING MY NORI GREEN LEXUS as far away from any other car as possible, I walk the three blocks toward the entrance to the Wesley Auction House situated on the courthouse square next to the legendary Almost Home restaurant. I see twinkling lights and hear soothing music from within. My talented friend Professor Eric Edberg is entertaining the crowd with enchanting cello music. He and I are very good buddies having worked together on the Greencastle Summer Music Festival for years, and I'll catch up with him later when he takes a break. Some people arrive wearing jeans and khakis, but most are decked out in splendid evening wear. After years of wearing suits and ties for work, I'm usually done with that attire, but tonight is a special occasion, so I've selected a trendy blue suit, a Countess Mara tie, handsome Italian leather shoes, and gold cufflinks. I look pretty sharp, if I do say so myself!

Both Kaylan and Emily are situated by the entrance greeting guests and checking for reservations. The mood is very festive, and I feel good about participating in the auction which will be held tomorrow morning both here and online. This preview event is meant to tantalize folks with fascinating objects that'll be sold, and to showcase Wesley's active role in Greencastle's thriving art community. I catch up with Marla who's chatting with our good friends the Engelstads and the Hunters who already have their cocktails.

The room is arranged with round tables for eight people, skirted with black tablecloths bearing Wesley's logo. Lining the walls are rectangular tables displaying the auction items. It's clear that this isn't Wesley's first rodeo. They know what they're doing.

I see Kat across the room and excuse myself from our friends to go say hello to her.

"The room looks great, Kat, and you look lovely tonight too. Love your necklace!"

"Thanks, Nathan, I saw you and Marla when you came in, but I haven't had a chance to greet her personally yet." We walk together to view my cameras and other fascinating objects that'll be auctioned tomorrow. There is a plethora of very old photographs dating before the American Civil War, presidential letters, political campaign literature, and a wide variety of guns, swords, and other period collectibles.

"Impressive!" I say. I imagine these pieces will attract a lot of attention." From behind us, we both hear an unusual swooshing sound and turn to see an odd-looking chap puffing on a respiratory inhaler.

"Oh," I hear Kat say. "Is that you, Dr. Gleep? I didn't recognize you at first."

"Yes, it's me, Ms. Landrigan. I hear that a lot these days. I'm surprised that you remember me at all."

"Of course, I remember you, Mortimer. Nathan, I'd like you to meet my colleague from the

Indianapolis Visual History Museum, Dr. Mortimer Gleep."

I reach my hand out to shake his hand, but he makes no effort to take it. The awkward moment is compounded even more as Dr. Gleep looks at my hand dismissively then turns and walks away.

"That was odd," I say to Kat. "I don't think we did anything to offend him, did we?"

"No, it wasn't us, Nathan. Mortimer Gleep has a reputation for being a very bright historian, but one really weird dude."

We view a few more items together, and I feel a tap on my shoulder. I turn to see a dapper gentleman who I don't immediately recognize.

"Mike Kramer!" he says with a winning smile on his face.

"No way, Mike! I can't believe you came all the way from Vacaville. Did Patty come with you?"

"No, she wanted to come, but her parrot rescue group has a major fundraiser this weekend too. She sends her very best regards though."

I give him a big hug. "I'm delighted that you came, Mike. Do you know Kat? I think you told me that you've auctioned a few cameras with Wesley in the past."

"Yes, I do know Kat, but I've never had the pleasure of meeting her in person. It's great to finally meet you, Kat."

"Welcome to Greencastle, Mike. We're honored that you joined us. So, how do you two know each other?"

"About three years ago I bought an Expo Watch Camera from Mike on eBay and then proceeded to purchase some of the finest cameras in my collection from him over the next few years … and in the process we've become very good friends."

"All true!" Mike confirms. "Nathan and I speak on the phone frequently, and when he told me that he was going to auction a few cameras, I thought it would be a hoot to surprise him."

"Well, you certainly did that, Mike. The truth is, Kat, I've learned a ton about rare cameras from Mike, and yes, we've become fast friends along the way."

Marla catches up to us, and she finally gets to meet Kat whose praises I've sung ever since we agreed to work together.

"Well, it's a pleasure to meet you, Kat. Nathan is very particular about who he shares his antique cameras with, and your positive reputation precedes you."

"Thank you, Marla, I wish all of Wesley's clients were as pleasant to work with as your husband."

"And, who is this handsome gentleman?"

"Marla, I'm pleased to introduce you to Mike Kramer from California."

"Oh my goodness, the famous Michael Kramer! You are a legend in our home, but I think we need to have a little chat, sir, about all the cameras Nathan's purchased from you. Whenever Nathan closes his office door, I figure he's on the phone with you, and it's going to cost a lot of money."

We chat a little bit longer, and then Kat excuses herself. "I better ask everyone to take their seats, as I've prepared a few brief words regarding tomorrow's auction. Marla and I see that our friends the Engelstads and the Hunters have saved seats for us at their table, and we walk over to join them. Mike K. and I agree to get together again before he heads back to Vacaville.

Dr. Edberg stops playing a special piece entitled "Becoming Stardust" that I originally composed for harmonica that he helped me transcribe onto sheet music. He shoots me a quick wink, and the cacophonous sound of the partygoers subsides as Kat steps up to the podium.

"Good evening, everyone. I'm Kat Landrigan, VP for Wesley Auction House's Department of American Historical Ephemera and Early Photography. It is, indeed, a pleasure to welcome you here this evening, and I promise to keep my comments very brief. We hope that the offerings we've displayed tonight will spark your enthusiasm for tomorrow's auction, and my staff and I will be happy to answer any questions you may have. We know that several of you have traveled quite a distance to join us this weekend, and we hope our Greencastle hospitality and the lodging that we've reserved at the Doc's Inn and the Inn at DePauw exceed your expectations. Before I go any further, though, I want to recognize my co-workers, Kaylan, Emily, and Miriam who are the true heroes for putting together our auction and reception. As you can imagine, it takes a lot of work to do these events, so please thank them before you leave."

Kat then addresses the audience with a few details about registering and bidding tomorrow and then concludes. "So please feel free to eat, drink, and be merry this evening and bring your checkbooks, cash, and credit cards tomorrow so we can pay for this soiree! Wesley Auction House is delighted to have you join us! Thank you very much!"

The audience gives Kat a hearty round of applause, and Marla and I and our friends do as Kat suggests … we eat, drink, and are very merry. Finally, it's time to bid our friends and Kat a *bon nuit*, and I head for the door to go pick up our car. Once outside, I notice Dr. Mortimer Gleep again. He has an odd expression on his face and is puffing away on his inhaler again. He turns his back to me as I pass him.

Three minutes later I pull our car up to the auction house and retrieve my lovely wife whose hugging the Hunters and the Engelstads goodbye.

"Well, darlin', I hope you had a very good time this evening."

"I did, Nathan! We certainly live in a very nice and supportive community, but who's that creepy looking man standing by himself over there? He seems to be muttering to himself like he's got Tourette Syndrome or something." I look in the direction that she's pointing, roll my eyes, put the Lexus in gear, and drive away.

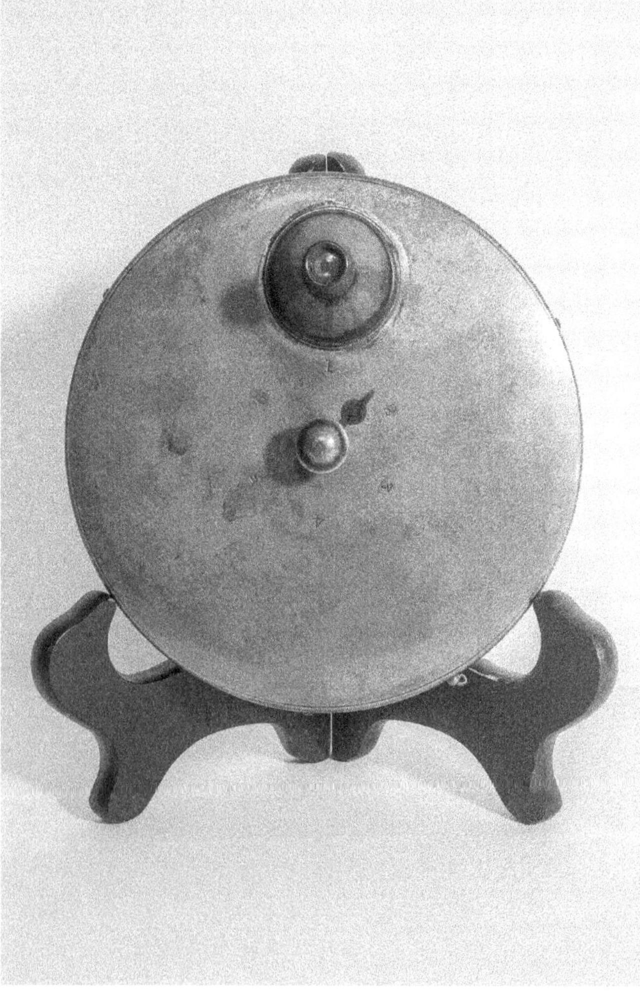

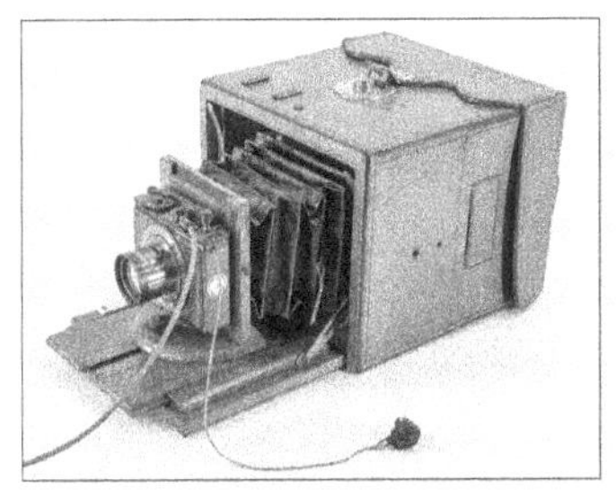

Chapter 13

"We made it!" I exclaim to Miriam, Emily, and Kaylan after the last guests have left the reception. We've hired a cleaning crew to come in and quickly get everything back in order. "Gee, and just think," Miriam sighs, "we'll be back here in less than ten hours to prepare for the actual auction."

"You guys have been awesome, so let's pack up our things and go home for a well-earned night's sleep. It's almost eleven and tomorrow will come soon enough."

Thankfully, the drive home to my cabin is easy. There's absolutely no traffic at this hour, and I've driven these country roads so much over the years that my car could probably steer itself. When I pull into my carport and go inside the cabin, Clover is waiting for me. I give him so fresh food and water, then hang up my party clothes, splash some water on my face, brush my teeth, and collapse into bed. Within minutes, I'm fast asleep and I dream of people and places long ago, and objects that I've helped auction over the years that connected me to many of those people and places. As an elfin maiden, sometimes it's hard to discern the blurry difference between then and now.

Then, sometime around 2:00 AM, I hear a sound that shatters my sleep. At first I'm not sure what it is, and then I realize it's my damn phone. "Who in the world would be calling me at this hour? This better be good." But, it's not ...

"Ms. Landrigan, this is Detective Shane calling. I'm terribly sorry to bother you at this hour, but there's been an incident, and we need you to return to town as soon as you're able."

"Incident?! What sort of incident?!" I ask sleepily.

"Well, ma'am, there's been a huge fire. It looks like arson, and the Wesley Auction House has been burned to the ground."

I'm virtually speechless trying to comprehend what I just heard. "Are you serious?" I ask. "How bad is it?" I implore.

"Like I said, ma'am, it's bad. The Greencastle Fire Department responded very quickly, and we were able to save the surrounding businesses, but I'm afraid that the Wesley Auction House is a total loss."

"I'll be right there, detective."

All the way into town, I think this can't possibly be happening. I know I need to contact our main office in Chicago but not at this hour. First, I need to survey the damage for myself and see what, if anything, is salvageable. As I approach the courthouse square, I see flashing lights from the first responders' vehicles. They light up the entire downtown, reflecting off other buildings. I park in front of the senior center a few doors away from our Wesley location, exit my car and stop dead in my tracks. Tears well up in my eyes and cascade down my cheeks as I see the extent of the damage. Like Detective Shane reported, it's bad.

I pass through a small gathering of curious onlookers and slowly approach what used to be our building. The scene is cordoned off with yellow tape, and firemen are scurrying here and there hosing down the last remnants of the fire. I duck under the yellow tape and am immediately stopped by one of the police officers.

"Sorry, ma'am, this is an active investigation scene, and I can't let you go in there." I see Detective Shane, and he motions for the officer to let me pass. Never in a million years would I ever have expected to see such total devastation.

"What do you know, detective? Any idea how this happened?"

"We won't know exactly how the fire started until our investigators complete their inspection, but it's fairly obvious that some sort of a chemical accelerant was used. I'm very sorry, Ms. Landrigan."

"Is it safe to look around, detective?"

"Not really, and we should stay out of the way and let our people do their jobs. Let's give it a few hours, okay?"

I nod my head affirmatively, but my mind is flooded with so many anxious thoughts and concerns, not just from a corporate liability standpoint, but also from the loss of so many historically important artifacts. "I can't believe this is happening," I murmur aloud.

"Yes, ma'am," Detective Shane replies sympathetically, and I bury my face into his chest and sob in ways I haven't done in centuries. He leads me away to a police cruiser, and a young officer hands me a blanket and cup of coffee to help keep the chill away. A few minutes later I hear my name called and see my three co-workers rushing to join me. All of us have tear-stained faces and look like we've just been mugged.

"You know, ladies, just yesterday I was thinking that our swan song auction would be memorable, but this is a memory that will haunt me forever."

An hour or so later, Detective Shane has interviewed the four of us, attempting to determine suspects and motives. Each of us is in so much shock that our replies are barely coherent.

"Well, we'd hired a cleaning crew to come in immediately after the reception was over so we could be ready for the auction today, but for the life of me, I can't imagine what motive they'd have. Besides, it's a family-run company that we've used for years and trust implicitly."

"I'll need the name of the owner and contact information for that company so we can interview them as well. Look, I know this is a very emotional time right now," Shane offers, "but any little details might be helpful."

Again, the four of us nod our understanding, but I don't think any of us are capable of truly understanding anything given the tragedy of it all.

"Can I go inside the ruins now, detective? I need to see if there's anything worth saving." He asks my co-workers to remain outside of the yellow crime scene tape, and he and I walk into the building's smoldering remains. The devastation is virtually total. What the fire didn't destroy, the water from the fire hoses finished the job. There are charred timbers, twisted metal, and broken glass everywhere. I walk over to a far wall that had display tables next to it and see a badly tarnished antique brass lens bearing the name Dallmeyer lying on the ground, no doubt from one of Nathan's cameras. I thought I was all cried out, but another stream of tears flow down my cheeks. "Oh, Nathan, I am so, so sorry."

The detective and I walk outside and rejoin my co-workers. He says, "There's nothing else the four of you can do here now. I'll be in touch with you immediately if something develops."

I nod and say, "C'mon ladies, let's walk over to the Bodega and see if we can get something to eat." As we walk, we begin making an initial list of calls we need to make, including my boss in Chicago, the consignors for what was to be today's auction, and the people whose art and artifacts we'd stored in the wareroom for upcoming online auctions that now will never occur.

"I hope you guys will stick by me with this. I wouldn't blame you if you walked away, given how corporate has treated you, but I . . . " The words catch in my throat."

Miriam looks at her two co-workers, and almost in unison they reply, "We've got your back, Kat.

You've always been there for us, and well, we stick together!" I give each of them a hug and say "thank you."

We glance over our shoulders at the location that used to be Wesley Auction House. "We're obviously going to need some temporary office space. Miriam, would please give Eric Wolfe a call? He'll take care of us."

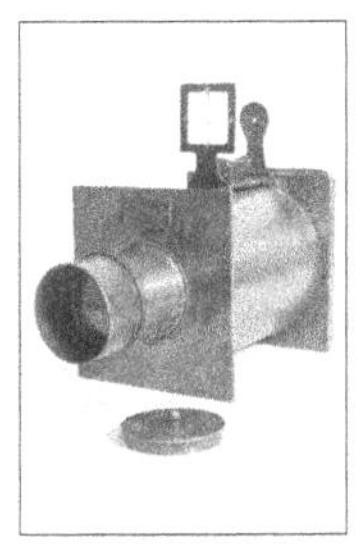

Chapter 14

A S WE'RE FINISHING OUR BREAKFAST at the Bodega, the owners, Joel and Tosh, come out from the kitchen and express their sympathies. "As small business owners we understand the challenges that face us every day. Even on a good day, it's still hard work. Wesley Auction House has been a landmark company in our community since way before we were born, and we just want you to know that we're here if you need us. We're so sorry you have to go through this tragedy. We're going to take sandwiches and drinks over to the first responders. They've got to be exhausted!"

"Thanks, guys. That means so much to us, and I'm sure the police and firefighters will be extremely grateful."

With our bellies full, we get up to part company. "I'll be in touch with you very soon, and we'll decide on next steps. Thank you so much again!

"What are you going to do now?" Kaylan asks.

"Well, as much as I want to go home and bury my head beneath the covers, there's someone I need to tell in person."

"Nathan?" Emily asks.

"Yeah, I want him to hear about it from me first."

We go our separate ways for now, and I walk back to my car. Along the way I see the first responders still hard at work with a huge crowd of townspeople looking at the aftermath of the conflagration. City sanitation workers and several volunteers help remove some of the trash that spilled onto the sidewalk and into the street. It's a total mess, and I know that Wesley Auction House and their insurance companies are going to have a huge financial bill to cover all of the losses, all for a location that Wesley had planned on shuttering soon. As I leave town on Highway 231 North, I call Nathan.

"Good morning, Kat, that was a special party last night. Are you calling to bask in the glory of last evening's festivities?"

"I wish I were, Nathan. I'd like to come out and see you if you have some time."

"That sounds a little ominous. Is everything okay?"

"Not really."

"So, when do you want to come?"

"Oh, say in about fifteen minutes." We hang up, and I accelerate up Water Works Hill heading toward County Road 250 North. Along the way I try to imagine who would want to burn our business to the ground. To my knowledge my team and I have always treated our clients graciously. In fact, we go overboard to ensure that our customers are very happy with their experiences with Wesley Auction House. And then, I remember the phone calls from Mr. Creepy. I'd been so engrossed with the tragedy of the fire that I'd forgotten about those threatening calls. I pick up my phone again and call Detective Shane. My call is sent to his voicemail. "Detective, I believe we may have a suspect. Please call me when you get this message."

By the time I arrive at Nathan's home, I've managed to calm down a bit mainly because I'm trying to remain professional and proactive rather than being a victim. He's standing on his back porch when I pull into his driveway. This time when I exit my car I don't feel the *lightness of being* that I felt on my two previous visits. As an elf I usually have a very good sense of myself and my surroundings, but right now I might as well be just another mere mortal.

Nathan sees the serious look on my face and says, "C'mon in. Marla's got some fresh coffee brewing, and we have plenty to eat if you're hungry."

"Thanks, Nathan, but just coffee would be fine."

Marla greets us in the kitchen, and I just blurt it out, "After the reception last night, someone set our building on fire and burned it to the ground with everything in it. I got called to the site about 2:00 AM and haven't returned home yet. I've spent the last several hours in town with the police and my exhausted staff. I wanted to drive out to see you so you heard about it from me first instead of on Facebook or Paul's Scanner."

"Oh, Kat, I'm so sorry. Was anyone injured in the fire?"

"No, nobody was hurt, but everything, including your cameras, is a total loss. I promise you, Nathan, that our insurance will cover all of the losses. We'll just need some time to get everything sorted out."

"Well, the good news is that no one was hurt, and while I'm not happy about losing the cameras, they are 'things' after all, and frankly they weren't my finest pieces. I'm more concerned about you right now. Do the police have any leads?"

"Nothing firm, but I may have a suspect that Detective Shane and I have discussed before."

"Whew, I'm pretty much at a loss for words, Kat. I'm not sure what we can do, but Marla and I would be happy to help in any way we can."

"Thank you both. That means a lot."

"I'm sure you need to contact a lot of people about this. If you need some office space, you're more than welcome to use mine until you get situated."

"Thanks, Nathan, Miriam plans to call Eric Wolfe in a bit to see if he's got some space that we could rent temporarily, but that could take a few days to arrange."

"Seriously, Kat, you are more than welcome to use my office. You won't be in our way, and you can have as much privacy as you need."

"You know, that's really a very generous offer, and that would be extremely helpful. The internet connection at my cabin is unreliable at times, so I think I'd like to take you up on that."

And, Marla offers, "We have plenty of guest space here if you just want to bunk with us for a while."

"You're very kind to suggest that, but all of my clothes are at home, and my bunny, Clover, relies on me, plus I honestly think I'll need some alone time at home to process everything that's swirling around in my head."

"We totally understand. Why don't you bring your coffee with you, and we'll get you settled in my office."

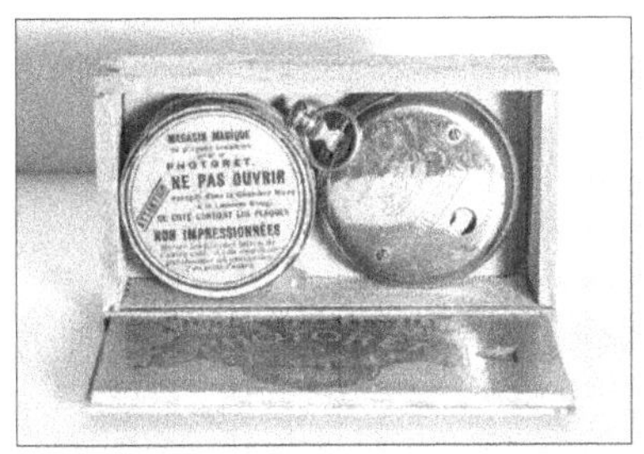

Chapter 15

THE MOMENT we step into Nathan's office that sensation of a *lightness of being* that I've experienced before, both here and in his driveway, returns to me. Everywhere I look I don't just see his antique cameras situated on shelves and tables, I see a virtual aura around each with shimmering images of people and places from years gone by. As an elf I've experienced many visual illusions over the centuries, but never with the clarity of these. It's like Nathan's office and his cameras are a portal to the past. I can't explain why. It's part of the mysteries of the elfin world that I've grown to accept. Nathan sees me looking around the room as if in a trance and asks, "Are you okay, Kat?"

"Huh?" I absently reply. "Oh, yeah, I think so. I guess I'm still in a state of shock from the fire, plus feeling somewhat sleep deprived, and I'm a little overwhelmed thinking about all of the people I need to contact today. Our Chicago office should be open now, and I dread telling my boss the horrible news, and of course I have a ton of folks who've consigned artifacts with us that my team and I need to communicate with. A lot of work facing us ... "

"I understand. I'll leave you to it, but if there's anything Marla and I can do to help, don't hesitate to say something, okay?"

I nod my head vacantly and say, "okay," and Nathan closes his office door to give me privacy. I take a sip of my coffee and try to focus on priorities. My first call is to Wesley's CEO, Peaches Panache, whose day I'll ruin from the get go. We talk at length, and I give her as much information as I can, including Detective Shane's contact information. Somehow Peaches seems to maintain her professional composure and tells me that Wesley's legal counsel and insurance agent will be in Greencastle before the end of the day. We agree that I should pursue temporary office space and see if my staff is willing to stay on until we get things under control.

"I think they will, but the company should seriously increase their severance packages given that they're not feeling much loyalty to a company that's informed them of their dismissal." Peaches agrees and asks me to please relay her sincere appreciation.

"I will, and I'll keep you posted on any information that comes my way. Now, I need to start making some calls to our consignors for today's, uh, *canceled* auction and the other consignors whose art and artifacts we held in the wareroom for upcoming sales." We hang up, and I sit brokenhearted, looking around Nathan's office.

Then, the quiet is shattered by my phone ringing. I'm hopeful that it's Detective Shane returning my earlier call, but it's one of the consignor's calling me about the fire. He seems to be reasonably sympathetic, but after him there are a steady stream of calls, a few of which are from clients who are understandably royally pissed off at their losses, some threatening nasty lawsuits. There's not a lot I can say to those folks other than that Wesley Auction

House will make good on their losses. I imagine our legal counsel would prefer that I not make any promises until the investigation is completed, but screw that!

My next call is from Miriam informing me that she's spoken with Eric Wolfe about temporary office space, and that he'll find something as quickly as possible, even if it means using some of his own Prime Real Estate office space. That's a relief.

The next phone call is from Detective Shane. "Hello, Kat, your message said you think you may have a possible suspect."

"Yes. You remember those two phone calls we received from that creepy man making threats about our company and its clients?"

"I do, and I'd been thinking about him as well. We were never able to get much in the way of reliable evidence, but I've already asked the phone company to put a trace on any other calls you may receive. I should've gotten your permission first, but given the level of tragedy you've suffered, I didn't think you'd mind."

"Yeah, that's fine, detective. Any avenue that helps us get to the bottom of this is welcome. Have your officers or the firefighters come up with any helpful tangible evidence?"

"Not really, Kat. As you know, the destruction was massive. I wish I could give you something, but we don't have anything to really go on at this point, other than knowing it was definitely arson."

"Okay then, let's keep in touch. I've spoken with our CEO, Peaches Panache, and given her your contact information for our legal counsel and insurance people. I'm sure you'll hear from them very soon." We hang up.

It's at tragic moments like these that I tend to take stock of my life, or should I say *my lives* since my elfin DNA has kept me viable through so many centuries. Everyone I've ever known has come and gone, and my work at Wesley Auction House, selling antique collectibles, has been my way of connecting and preserving the past with the present. I've always loved my work which has been my mainstay since I never raised children of my own. My dear lover, Henri, and I had dreamed of creating our own family, but alas, my elfin genetics and his never worked biologically, and believe me, it wasn't for a lack of effort on our part. Such is life . . .

The phone is quiet for now, and I look around Nathan's office, seeing marvelous antique cameras and photographs that I'd not closely examined before because he has so many. Now, with my mind a little more at ease, I see true treasures of photographic history, each with stories to tell. They also give me insights into Nathan's approach to collecting. Over time I've curated so many collections that are hodgepodges of stuff. Many collectors are hoarders who see things and just buy them for the sake of adding to their trove. Nathan, on the other hand, has brought a systematic approach to studying the early timeline of photography, and I admire the way he's built his collection.

Of particular note are Nathan's three Daguerreotype cameras that are in remarkable condition. I gently lift his American Chamfered Box Daguerreotype camera from its original wooden tripod and cradle it in my hands. It dates to within the first ten years of photography's *invention*. Immediately, it acts as a portal to the past, and I see a vision of a gentleman in a Boston photography studio having his portrait taken. It's a thrill to see the period attire that the photographer and his stiff-looking subject are wearing and the decor in the gallery. Next, I pick up Nathan's French Daguerreotype camera, and I'm virtually whisked away to an outdoor scene somewhere in the south of France. It's a mesmerizing experience, one that makes me long for when Henri and I would travel the countryside together, loving the adventure and each other.

I then pick up a few of Nathan's antique detective-style cameras such as his Gray's Vest camera and his Photoret Watch camera that gave a photographer opportunities to take candid photos of unsuspecting people. On and on I pick up various cameras, and each time I travel back in time to places and people who experienced the wonder of having their portraits taken. In a few instances, though, the experience is actually quite horrific, seeing dead soldiers lying in grotesque positions during the American Civil War.

And, then I see the marvelous camera made by Jean Guido Sigriste in Paris around 1900. It's the same camera I held on a previous visit to Nathan's home and was virtually reconnected with Henri. I'm hopeful that I can repeat that happenstance, and the moment I look into the camera's viewfinder I'm magically swept away to a vibrant Parisian street scene and see Henri's smiling face and arms beckoning me to join him. Tears well up in my eyes, and my heart melts at the very thought of his presence. "Oh, Henri . . . if only we could . . . "

I hear Nathan lightly knock on his office door and see him peek through the doorway. "I'm sorry to interrupt, Kat, but Marla and I are going to have some lunch and wanted to know if you'd like to join us." He sees me holding the Sigriste and says, "Incredible camera, huh?!"

"Indeed, it is. Truly magical!" I reluctantly set the camera aside, and say, "Yes, lunch would be great. I suddenly find that I'm famished as if I've traveled the world. I'd love to join you. Thanks!"

We enjoy a very tasty salad that Marla prepared from vegetables she's grown in their garden, and I find myself nourished and very grateful for their warm hospitality. "I think I've done as much as I can this morning and feel a need to get back to my cabin to check on things, but I'd love to return later, if that's okay. You guys have been great!"

"Of course!" Marla replies. "You're always welcome in our home."

After we work together cleaning up the kitchen, Nathan walks me to the door. "Kat, I'm really pleased that you appreciate the antique cameras as much as you do. To me, there's always been something very special about them, aside from their physical beauty. It's hard to describe, but it's as if I can feel *transported* in time by them. I know that sounds nutty, but they're not just collectible objects to me. They sometimes feel like portals to different moments in time."

I look directly into Nathan's eyes. "There's nothing *nutty* about it, Nathan. These are sensations that very few people recognize, and even fewer people understand. I'm not sure that I totally understand them either, but I'm grateful that this is something that we can share because it's very lonely seeing other realities that most people simply disregard like fleeting thoughts. Perhaps we can speak more about this later."

"Until later then," he replies.

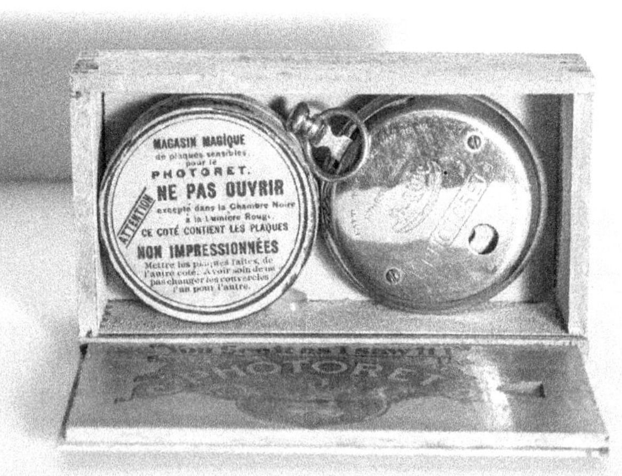
MAGASIN MAGIQUE
de plaques sensibles
pour le
PHOTORET.
NE PAS OUVRIR
ATTENTION excepté dans la Chambre Noire
à la Lumière Rouge.
CE COTÉ CONTIENT LES PLAQUES
NON IMPRESSIONNÉES
Mettre les plaques faites, de
l'autre coté. Avoir soin de ne
pas changer les couvercles
l'un pour l'autre.
PHOTORET

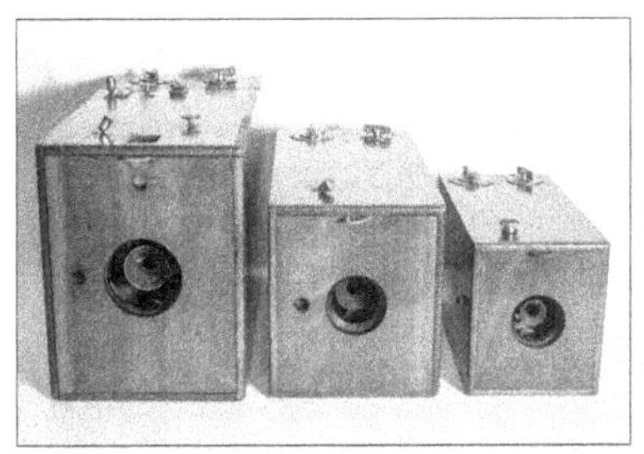

Chapter 16

THANK GOODNESS the drive back to my cabin is absent of any significant traffic because my mind is flying in so many directions at one time: The fire, the lost livelihoods of my co-workers, the mystery surrounding the cameras, and of course my connecting with Henri again after so many years. I'm relieved when I finally arrive home, comforted by the friendship of my woodland friends and the sanctity of the ever-flowing river of time that is Big Walnut Creek.

As I open the cabin door, Clover comes rushing to greet me. He's so excited that he leaps up into my arms and nuzzles my neck.

"I know, I know, I missed you too, sweet boy. You act as if I was never returning, but I'd never forget you." I put fresh lettuce and carrots in his bowl and give him cool drinking water. He munches loudly, and I build a fire in the woodstove to keep the autumn chill at bay. Then, I do what any exhausted elfin maiden would do. I collapse into bed, fully clothed, and lie staring at the ceiling until sleep finally overtakes my wakefulness ... and I dream ...

I see fragments of my life in crystal clarity. Images of people and places that I've known over many years appear briefly and morph as if in a kaleidoscope. I recall my youth as an adolescent elf being taught our mystical ways, how we're different from mortals, and why it's important to live righteously without revealing our magical heritage. Faces appear in my dreams that I haven't thought about for centuries, friends mixed with casual acquaintances, people whose lives I briefly shared and then were gone. I see princes and paupers, city dwellers and simple country folk. I see great artists whose creations celebrate the greatness that humankind can ascend to, and I witness the horrors of war, pestilence, and famine. And, I see my life in present day, my fulfilling work and energetic colleagues at Wesley Auction House, my morning walks along Big Walnut Creek with my woodland friends, and my unexpected connections with Nathan's cameras. And, as with most aspects of life, I see the heartbreaking tragedies that also occur along the way, the recent fire and the devastating losses.

And then I awake with Clover by my side, snoozing as if he doesn't have a care in the world, and I wish that my life was that simple. As I lie in bed looking at the camera obscura effect of the pine tree through the knothole on my bedroom wall, it dawns on me how alike reality and fantasy can be, how very similar dreams and real life often are. Who's to say that the magical images I experience in Nathan's office are any different than the *magic* that occurs in normal, human life. "It's all in the eye of the beholder," I murmur to myself.

I gently nudge Clover who's not in any hurry to move away from the warmth of my body. "C'mon, buddy, this elfin maiden has things I need to do, and lying here dreaming isn't gonna get the work done."

We both hop to the floor, and I prepare a pot of coffee to help ramp up my wakefulness, and then my phone rings. "Let the fun begin!" I mutter sarcastically.

"Hello, this is Kat." At first the caller on the other end is silent, although I hear labored breathing. "Hello," I say again, without an immediate reply. I'm about to hang up when I hear words that chill me.

"So, Ms. Landrigan, that sure was a hot time in the old town last night, eh?!"

"Who is this?" I demand.

"Oh, someone, uh, very naughty! Someone who feels righteously victorious and cleansed by the purity of fire."

"That's a rather psychotic way of putting it. Don't you think? A lot of innocent people were hurt by your ugliness."

"C'est la vie, my dear Ms. Landrigan! Someone needed to teach you and your mercenary colleagues and greedy collectors a lesson about enriching yourselves through the sales of historic artifacts."

"You need psychiatric help, asshole! Better yet, you need a solitary cell someplace far away from decent people."

"You may be right, Ms. Landrigan, but what makes you think my life already isn't confined to a deep, dark cell?!"

"Who are you?" I demand again. "You know the authorities and my company will never rest until you're put away for good."

"Well, good luck with that you prim little dilettante! And, don't think for a second that I'm finished with my retribution! I know where you live." Then, there's a vague puffing sound, and the caller hangs up.

I stare angrily at the phone and then call Detective Shane.

"Well, it appears we still have a problem, detective. I just received a threatening call from Mr. Creepy. It appears we're not rid of him yet. He says he knows where I live. You might want to check my recent phone log and see if we can collar this sonovabitch before he acts again."

"I'll see what I can do, and in the meantime I'll assign a couple of officers to watch your home."

Some sixty miles away in Indianapolis, Dr. Mortimer Gleep sneers and snorts in the musty confines of his office deep in the Visual History Museum. He approaches the mirror in his office and examines his visage, looking closely at his snow white hair pulled back in a pony tail, his long, scruffy white beard, and hollow pale blue eyes. "Well, you're not gonna win any beauty contests, are ya, Mortie, my boy?! But, at least I *built a fire* under those snooty people at Wesley Auction House, and best of all, I got away with it! Got their attention, didn't I?!"

He saunters triumphantly out of his office and goes down the hallway to a basement utility room and takes stock of its contents. "Seems like I've got just enough ammonium nitrate for one last conflagration." He loads it carefully into canisters and lifts them onto a cart. Then, he wheels it to the museum's loading dock and carefully places them inside an unmarked panel van. "Yup, this should do the trick! Just need to wait until dark and take a nice little drive into the country along Big Walnut

Creek. I reckon my work's not done until the Kat Lady sings . . . or cries!"

His laughter echoes throughout the museum, but it's after hours, and no one is around to hear it.

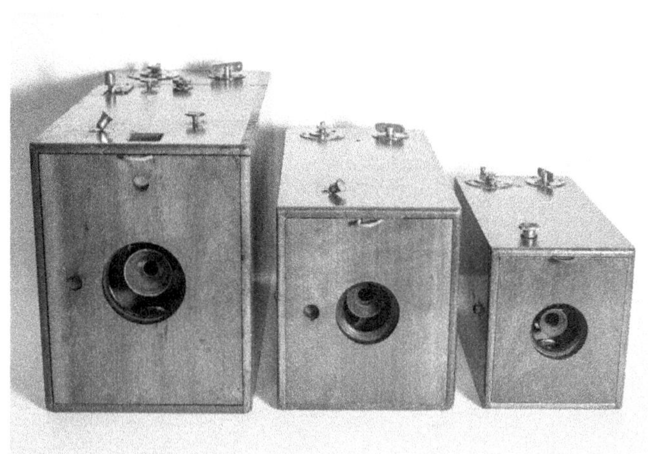

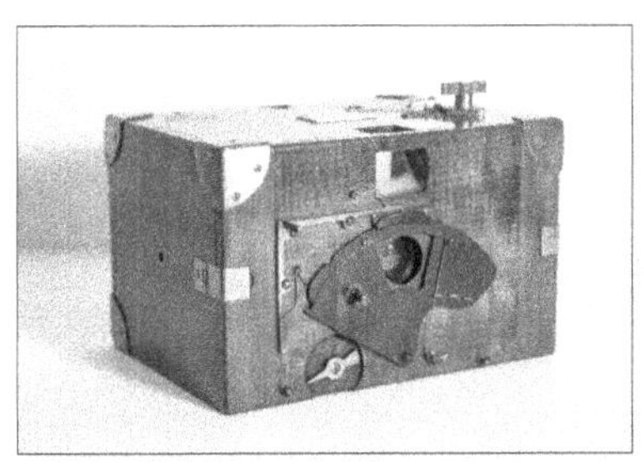

Chapter 17

AFTER HAVING MY COFFEE and a light meal, I give Nathan a call to see if I can spend more time in his office.

"Sure, Kat, c'mon over. We're just finishing up dinner, but we have plenty left if you're hungry."

"Thanks, Nathan, but I just had something. How 'bout I drop by in about forty-five minutes? From our last conversation by your back door, it seems that we share a common, uh, curiosity about the portal-power of your cameras."

"Yeah, I think so too. See you soon!"

After we hang up, I freshen up and change clothes. "Okay, Mister Clover, you're in charge while I'm gone, okay? Don't let any nasty guys in, and please be nice to the police officers when they get here." Clover stands up on his hindquarters as if to acknowledge his marching orders. Given the hour, the sun is beginning to set, and I pass a police cruiser heading to my cabin. It's a relief to see that Detective Shane has my back.

I arrive at Nathan's house several minutes later and watch him arranging his rakes and yard tools in his garden shed. Given my life as an elf, I've always avoided getting too close to most humans because I know there will come a time when they age and pass away, and it's very difficult for me to say goodbye to dear friends. In his case, though, I feel a fond connection with Nathan, not in any sort of sexual way, but as a comrade who shares very similar interests with me. It's rare for me, and I'm grateful for his friendship. I exit my car and once again feel that sensation of a *lightness of being* that tells me this place is special, a corridor to other realms. Why it is that way, I do not know, nor do I really care. I try to just accept what is and deal with what those sensations offer me.

"Greetings!"

"Back at ya, Kat! I hope you've had a productive day."

"Yeah, not exactly how I wanted to spend my day, but I've managed to get over the initial shock of last night. I really appreciate you and Marla sharing your time and home with me. It's a mitzvah . . . a good deed . . . as an old rabbi friend of mine used to say."

"C'mon in. How about a glass of wine, or something stronger if you prefer?"

"Ya know, a good snort of bourbon could be just what the doctor ordered. Whatever you've got handy!"

"Coming right up. Marla likes Bulleit bourbon so we always keep a supply in the liquor cabinet. I personally think all alcohol tastes like poison, but tonight I'll resist my puritanical ways and join you nonetheless."

"Is Marla home? Maybe she'd like to join us in a glass of 80 proof poison?"

She would, but she's meeting some girlfriends at the Whisk. Joel and Tosh are performing some new tunes, and she'll be home later."

We go into the den, pour ourselves a generous amount, and head back up to his office.

"So, have the police been able to get any leads on who started the fire last night?"

"Nothing definite, so far, but I got phone call about an hour ago from the prick, celebrating the destruction. It's pretty unsettling, and I have a feeling he's not finished yet."

"Have you notified the authorities?"

"Yeah, I have, and they're on it. Candidly, there's this jerk who apparently hates people in my profession and savvy collectors such as you. He's made some threatening calls in the past, but I always assumed he was just weird, but not dangerous."

"Oh, I wonder if I need to drag my shotgun out just in case."

"May not be a bad idea, Nathan, but he seems to be especially focused on me and Wesley Auction House."

Simultaneously, we both take a snort of Bulleit. Nathan shudders as it goes down.

"So, where were we? What do you want to look at next, Kat?

"So, tell me about these cameras that have multiple lenses. Some have four, some have six, and some have nine lenses or more."

"Without boring you to death, photographers used them so they could take more than one picture at the same time. It enabled them to be more efficient and sell more pictures without having to take individual shots."

"Makes sense." Nathan hands me a gorgeous quarter-plate camera with four lenses that was made by a maker named Rouch in London about 1860.

The camera seems to glow as I hold it in my hands and shortly thereafter I feel like I'm transported back in time to a studio in nineteenth-century London.

Nathan watches closely as I appear to be mesmerized by what I'm experiencing. I feel like I'm wearing contemporary virtual reality goggles and appear to be in a SoHo garret studio illuminated by natural light pouring in through skylights. The photographer affixes a head clamp to the back of the subject's neck to hold him steady during the long exposure, and then the photographer slips a dark cloth over his head to block out extraneous light as he focuses on the ground glass. He opens the camera's flap shutter, and eight seconds later the exposure is complete.

"Amazing," I murmur aloud. "Simply amazing!"

Nathan watches me closely as I seem transfixed by what I just experienced.

"So, where were you just now, Kat? You seemed to be lost in thought in another time and place."

I look into Nathan's eyes plumbing the depths of his friendship with me, and for the first time since I once told Henri, I decide to share the secret of my elfin life.

"I wish to tell you something, Nathan, that I haven't shared with anyone for a long, long time. It's deeply personal and frankly you may find it a bit bewildering."

"Okay," he says curiously. We both take a generous sip from our glasses and sit down. "I hope you know that you can trust me, Kat. Whatever it is you wish to share will stay with me, okay?"

"I'm an elf, and I've lived for hundreds of years."

He begins to laugh and says, "That's a good one, Kat, and I'm seven feet tall and play center for the Indiana Pacers!" We both begin laughing at the hilarity of it all, and then he looks at me and says, "You're serious, aren't you?"

I nod my head affirmatively, and he takes another pull on his drink. "If that's true, and I always suspected that you were, uh, unique, what more do you feel comfortable sharing?"

Over the next hour I tell Nathan everything about my age, my upbringing as an elf maiden, the special powers that I possess, why I chose the profession that I did, and my ability to hold his cameras and have them become portals to the past. At the end of that hour, and after answering his thoughtful questions, I feel like a weight has been lifted off my shoulders, that I have finally been liberated . . .

"Whoa! That's something I didn't see coming, but I'm flattered and honored that you shared who and what you are with me, and I promise to protect your privacy." To help lighten the moment, though, I joke about our going to Las Vegas and playing roulette and blackjack. "No, seriously, Kat, I'm very honored that you shared that with me, and I respect you even more for it."

We chat more about my life and my experiences holding the cameras. It's clear that holding the Sigriste camera helped connect me to someone who was, and will forever be, the love of my life.

By the end of the evening, I've held several more of Nathan's cameras, and from his seat he sees that I'm virtually transported back in time. Nathan is careful not to say anything during those moments for fear of interrupting something so personal and magical. After each transformation, I smile and briefly share what occurred. It is an incredible experience for Nathan that reminds him that hubristic humans do not know everything about different dimensions in our world.

"Nathan, I must say that I feel emotionally drained, not in a bad way, though, and I'm very glad this was something we could share together."

A few moments later we hear Marla call upstairs to us. "Are you guys still talking about cameras, and I see you got into the bourbon!"

"Of course! We'll be down in a minute, okay?"

"Anything else you care to talk about, Kat?"

"Probably a ton of things, but I think I've pretty much exhausted everything that immediately comes to mind. Thank you for being such a good listener, Nathan."

"My pleasure, Kat, and like I said, your *specialness* will remain our secret."

We go downstairs and join Marla. "I had a great time tonight at the Whisk. Joel and Tosh wowed the audience with wonderful new songs and a few classic cover tunes. I take it you guys entertained yourselves too."

"Yeah, it was a fun evening. We're just a pair of old camera geeks enjoying the history of photography." I smile at Nathan and he winks back.

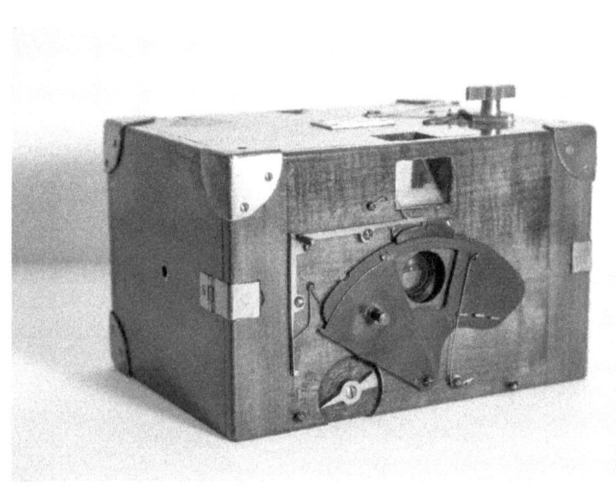

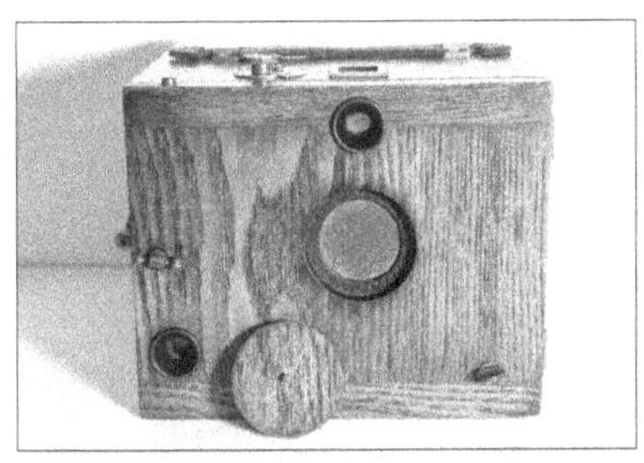

Chapter 18

THE SUN IS WELL BELOW THE HORIZON as Dr. Mortimer Gleep slowly drives the museum's van loaded with canisters containing highly flammable ammonium nitrate and fuel oil. He'd had no difficulty acquiring the main ingredients found in fertilizer from a local farm supply store a few days earlier. He heads north on Highway 231 and takes an exit leading him to the secluded road that runs along Big Walnut Creek. He'd managed to find Kat's home address listed in the local phone directory and is slowly meandering his way to that location.

As he approaches her cabin, he notices a police cruiser sitting in her driveway. "Hmm, it appears that good 'ol Kat has taken my warnings seriously, but why wouldn't she since I burned her precious building to the ground? It appears I need to create a diversion."

Mortimer drives past Kat's home and spies an old wooden barn about two miles away. It's filled with recently harvested hay and straw. He pulls the van behind the barn and carefully unloads one of the canisters. He drags it inside and sets a timer for one minute, adequate time for him to remotely explode the contents and drive a safe distance away. And, that's what he does.

As the barn is engulfed in flames, he calls the Putnam County emergency services number to report the fire.

"Yeah, I'm driving along Big Walnut Creek, and there's a big barn that's on fire. You might want to get some first responders out here to make sure it doesn't spread to nearby homes."

The call goes out to the volunteer fire department in Roachdale and other first responders near that location. The two police officers keeping watch on Kat's property hear the report on their radio and know they're only a short distance away. With lights flashing, they immediately respond to the call. Mortimer watches as the cruiser goes flying by him, and he steers the van to Kat's cabin.

"Can't dawdle, Mortie, my boy! No telling when these geniuses will return." He backs the van to the cabin's front door, kicks it open, sending Clover scurrying for cover, and hauls two canisters inside and leaves one on the front porch. He rushes back to the van and skedaddles out to the road where he waits briefly and presses the buttons on his remote device. A moment later Kat's cozy cabin is engulfed in orange flames, lighting up the night sky for miles. "Yup, that should do it! Now, I gotta get the hell outta here!"

Several minutes later back at Nathan and Marla's home, Kat is preparing to leave when her phone rings. She see that it's Detective Shane calling and she answers it. "What's the good word, detective?"

"Nothing good, Kat. Your cabin's on fire. Wherever you are, you should meet me there."

"I'm less than fifteen minutes away, detective. How bad is it?"

"Not good."

When I approach my driveway, I see that my home is nearly a total loss. Any first responders that might've been available to extinguish the flames are dealing with the barn fire two miles away. For the second time in two days I witness a loss of something very precious to me. The sadness and anger I feel is overwhelming. As I exit my car, I see Detective Shane pull his cruiser behind me. He sees me heading for my cabin and immediately rushes to me. He pulls me away. "You can't go in there, Kat!"

"But, my rabbit was inside. I need to save Clover!" I begin calling Clover's name praying that he's safe. I call and I call, but he doesn't appear. "Oh, Clover! My sweet, sweet friend. Where are you?!"

Detective Shane stands silently beside me as we watch my lovely home disappear into a heap of ash and cinders.

"I'm so sorry, Kat! I promise you we'll get the sonovabitch who did this."

"Well, he better hope that you find him first, because I'm not about to show any mercy if I get my hands on him." I have never been so angry in my life."

A couple of minutes later I see a Lexus pull into the driveway, and Nathan and Marla exit and join us. No one speaks. We all just stare in total disbelief. Shortly thereafter, a few members of the local volunteer fire department arrive, but by that time it's too late. My cozy cabin is a total loss. I thought that all of my tears had been used up with last night's fire, but a steady stream cascades down my face. "You bastard!" I hurl into the universe. I walk around to the rear of where my lovely cabin once stood, and hear a soft mew. I turn and see Clover hiding under a bush, and we rush to each other. "Oh, my sweet boy, I thought I lost you!" His fur is a little singed, but somehow he managed to escape the flames. He nuzzles my neck, and I hold him close, promising him I'll never leave him again.

I walk back to join the Andrews and Detective Shane and say, "Look who I found! It's my bestest friend, Clover. I thought I'd lost him."

"Well, you two obviously can't stay here, Kat. Why don't you and Clover come back to our place, and we can return tomorrow to see if any of your belongings survived."

I nod agreeably, and we finally decide to head back to their home. Detective Shane states that he'll remain on-site to supervise anything else that needs to be done, although in the dark not much is possible. I glance again at the horrible mess that used to be my wonderful home and gently place Clover in my car. Then, I look heavenward. "Is there no end to the cruelty that humans can do?"

The drive back to Nathan and Marla's house is brief, but along the way I see a lifetime of memories flash in my mind's eye. "I don't know, Clover, in some ways I feel like my work in the present day is done here. I guess it's true that everything and everyone eventually comes and goes. Even us, I reckon."

When I exit my car in their driveway, I feel that now familiar mystical sensation, and I take some solace believing in the eternal elfin ways.

Once inside, Nathan pulls out the bottle of bourbon and some cheese and crackers. Clover hops around as if he owns the place and revels in the fresh veggies and water that Marla provides. I look heavenward again and acknowledge that perhaps some humans are very kind-hearted after all.

It's been one helluva couple of days, and the Andrews get the guest bedroom set up for me and my bestest friend. Tomorrow's another day.

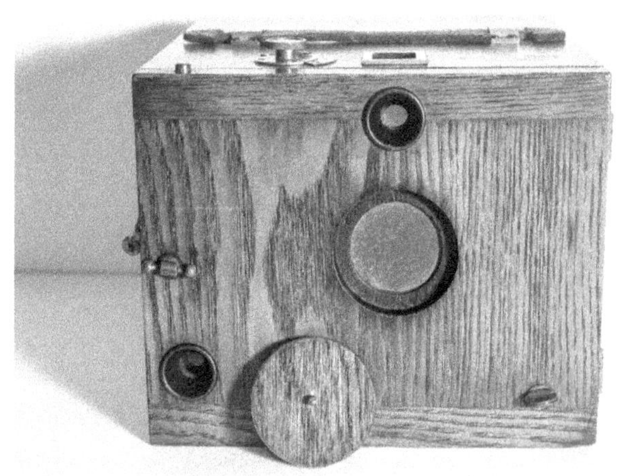

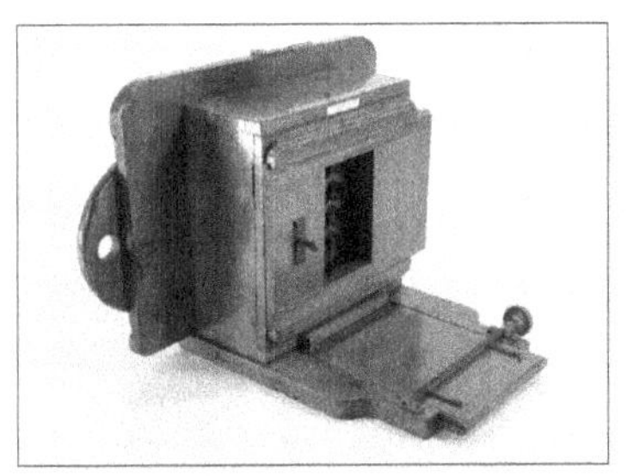

Chapter 19

AWAKE EARLY the next morning expecting to see the *camera obscura* effect of the inverted pine tree shining on my bedroom wall, then I remember that the cabin is now in ashes, and that I'll never see that same visual effect again. Clover is lying safely by my side, and I bend down to lightly kiss his head. The faint odor of singed fur reminds me of how close I came to losing him.

"C'mon buddy," I say to him. "Time to get up. We should let these good people have their privacy, and we need to see if there's anything we can retrieve at home." He leaps to the floor and goes racing into the kitchen to see if breakfast is available this morning.

As I approach the kitchen, I hear Marla say, "Well, good morning, Sir Bunny, and how did you sleep?" Clover surprises me by leaning against her leg and looking into her eyes. "Well, you really are the sweetest little fella, aren't you?!" She gives him a few pieces of cantaloupe and berries, and he's one happy hare.

"Good morning," I say as I enter the kitchen. "What can I do to help?"

"Nothing really. There's coffee ready for you, and I'll cook up some eggs and bacon once Nathan joins us. How'd you sleep?"

"Surprisingly well, thank you. I/we can't thank you enough for your hospitality can we, Clover?" He looks at me momentarily and then dives into another helping of succulent fruit.

"G'morning everyone!" Nathan voices as he enters the kitchen unshaven and his hair unkempt.

"Well, you just look a mess, darling!"

"Thank you, sweetheart!" he replies. "It's tough being an aging sex symbol!" We all laugh, and it helps set a lighter mood for what promises to be another very emotional day. We make idle chitchat during breakfast, and then Marla announces that she's teaching a yoga class in a little bit and needs to prepare. Nathan and I split the few remaining pieces of bacon, and I help clean up the breakfast dishes.

"Before you leave, Kat, would you like to come back upstairs to my office? There are a few exciting French cameras that we didn't get around to seeing."

"Sure, that would be great, but I can't stay too long. I'm anxious to get home and see what, if anything, survived the fire." We take our coffee cups upstairs and settle into the friendly confines of his office. No sooner do we sit down than my phone rings, and I answer it expecting it to be a call from Detective Shane. I put the phone on speaker so Nathan can hear our conversation.

"So, hello detective, you're on the job bright and early this morning. Any news to report?"

But, it's not the detective. "There you are, Ms. Landrigan, I was wondering if you enjoyed my little *fireworks* at your home last evening."

My blood runs cold, and it's everything I can do to keep my composure. "Well, I'm sure you're very proud of yourself. You've managed to destroy a lot of valuable property over the last two days, not to mention a mountain of hopes and dreams."

"Yes, alas, these things happen, don't they?" he smugly replies.

"So, what else do you want? I think you've already made whatever point you were eager to make."

"Yes, I believe I have. I just wanted to hear your voice one final time before I depart the area for good." Then, there's an vaguely familiar sound that changes everything ... a puffing, inhalation sound like from a rescue inhaler ... and the call ends.

Nathan and I stare at each other with an epiphany etched on both of our faces. "It's him, isn't it?" Nathan declares hopefully. "That pedantic, unscrupulous, rude sonovabitch!"

"I think so. Let's call Detective Shane!"

"Good morning, Kat, I hope you had a decent night's sleep, all things considered. Are you back at your property now?"

"No, I'm actually still at the Andrews' house, and you'll never guess who I just received a call from."

"Seriously, the arsonist just called you again? That guy sure likes to add fuel to the fire with his taunting. What'd he say? Anything revealing?"

"Nathan and I had his call on speakerphone so he can verify everything I heard."

"And?" the detective prompts.

"It wasn't so much what he said to me because it was basically the same bullshit taunting, but it was how he said it."

"I'm not sure I understand, Kat."

"Do you remember when the perpetrator first left a message on our phone at Wesley Auction House? You said your investigators thought he had a respiratory condition."

"Yeah, I recall that. So?"

"So, at the reception I was speaking with Nathan, and we were rudely interrupted by Dr. Mortimer Gleep who's a really weird curator in Indianapolis at the Visual History Museum. He repeatedly puffed on a respiratory inhaler that made a distinctive sound each time he took a puff on it."

"And, you think it's the same guy who burned the auction house and your cabin?"

"Nathan and I both do, and since we have no other leads to go on, we thought you might want to contact your counterparts in Indy and question this jerk. He told us he's about to leave town for good, so I think we need to hustle on this before he's in the wind, and we never catch him."

"I agree, Kat. I'll get right on it!"

"Nathan and I are going to meet you at that museum. We'll be there in an hour."

"This is police business, Kat, and I'm asking you to stand down until you hear back from me."

"No way, detective! After what this criminal has done, I'm definitely gonna be there to see the look on his face when you apprehend him. We'll see you there!"

Marla offers to look after Clover while we're away, and Nathan and I get into his Lexus and speed off to Indy. Morning rush-hour traffic is building, but Nathan deftly navigates it, which is a polite way of saying that he drove like a bat outta hell! About an hour later we slow our speed as we enter the Fountain Square area.

"There's the museum, Nathan, just up ahead." He pulls his car over to the curb across from the museum, and we impatiently wait for the authorities to arrive.

"Where are you, detective? We're in Nathan's green SUV across from the museum's entrance."

"I see your car, Kat, and the Indy police are sending multiple vehicles to assist. On the drive here, I alerted them to the situation. Please stay in your vehicle and let us do our jobs."

Within a few minutes, we see Indianapolis' *finest* arrive on the scene. Detective Shane speaks briefly with an Indy cop who directs a police cruiser to the rear of the museum.

Nathan and I watch anxiously as Detective Shane and two officers approach the main entrance to the museum which is closed because it's Sunday. "You want us to bust open the door, detective?"

"No, not yet. We've witnessed enough property damage over the past couple of days. Let me see if I can reach this guy on the phone, and we avoid any unnecessary drama."

Detective Shane phones the museum, not really expecting someone to answer, but Mortimer takes the call. "We're closed. Go away!" he blurts and then hangs up.

The detective chooses to call again, and Dr. Gleep replies again. "I said we're closed. Go the hell away!"

Before he hangs up again, the good detective announces, "Mortimer Gleep, this is Detective Shane from the Greencastle Police Department. We have some questions we need to ask you. Open the door immediately and surrender yourself!"

"Not gonna happen, detective!" Gleep drops the phone and runs down the hallway to the basement utility room and wheels one final canister of ammonium nitrate into the panel van which is parked inside the museum's loading dock.

"How about now, detective?" And Shane motions for the officer to bust through the front door. Nathan and I watch as the drama unfolds from inside his Lexus.

Nothing happens at first, and Nathan and I wonder if they found and apprehended the demonic curator. Then, we hear the enormous crushing sound of wood and steel being broken as Mortimer's van busts through the loading dock door and rams headlong into the front of the awaiting police cruiser. The officer is surprised by Mortimer's assault which renders the cruiser inoperable.

The next thing we see is an unmarked white panel van skid onto the street we're on and speed off in front of us.

"Holy shit!" Nathan hollers. "He's getting away!" He starts his car, and we take off in hot pursuit. I look behind us and see flashing lights from Detective Shane's car about a hundred yards behind us.

"Don't lose him, Nathan!"

Mortimer's van runs through a red light and then another, sideswiping another vehicle as he makes for I-70. Nathan runs the same red lights and closes the gap, and then we get lucky as we see smoke and steam coming from the damaged van which is crawling to a dead stop.

"We've got him, Kat!"

Then, we see the rear door of the van open, and Dr. Mortimer Gleep shoves his last explosive canister onto the pavement. He stands in the open door holding what presumably is a detonator. Detective Shane pulls up beside our car and is immediately followed by an Indy police cruiser.

Shane leaps out, with his service revolver in hand. "Give it up, Gleep, and no one gets hurt!"

Mortimer takes what appears to be a puff on his inhaler and detonates the canister. The explosion is deafening and orange flames burst windows and doors for a city block. The force of the detonation hurls the detective onto the hood of his car, and we see Mortimer limping and trying to get away on foot. The other officers rush to Shane's aid, and I open my car door in literally hot pursuit of the *futhermucker* who ruined my business and home.

Gleep manages to run about a hundred yards before my spry elfin legs catch up to him, and I leap and roughly toss his sorry ass to the ground. His long white hair and scraggy beard are covered in singed grime, and his pale blue eyes stare vacantly in shock. A moment later two cops join me and shackle him in handcuffs. The nightmare is finally over.

I see Nathan standing next to an ambulance that just arrived as they tend to Shane's injuries which are largely superficial. He looks at me, and smiles. "You're something else, Kat Landrigan. If it weren't for you and Mr. Andrews, this guy might've gotten away. The Indy cop says you virtually flew through the air to catch this guy."

"Well, we got lucky for a change, plus my adrenalin kicked in. Once Nathan and I figured out who the arsonist was, there was no way we were gonna let him get away." We linger on the scene long enough for me to confront Mortimer one last time, and to hear him make a full confession. I was assured that he would be put away in a deep, dark cell forever.

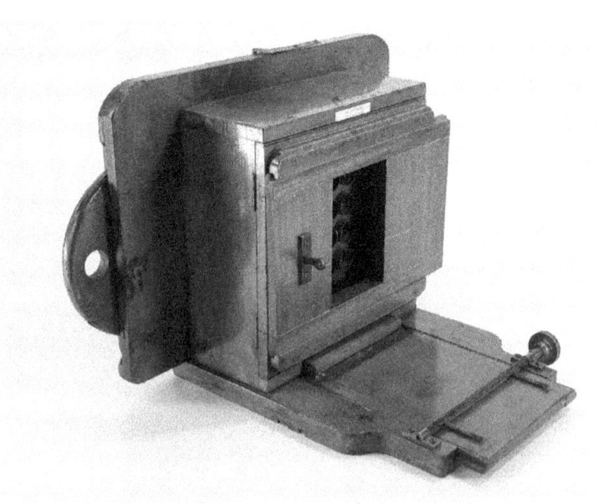

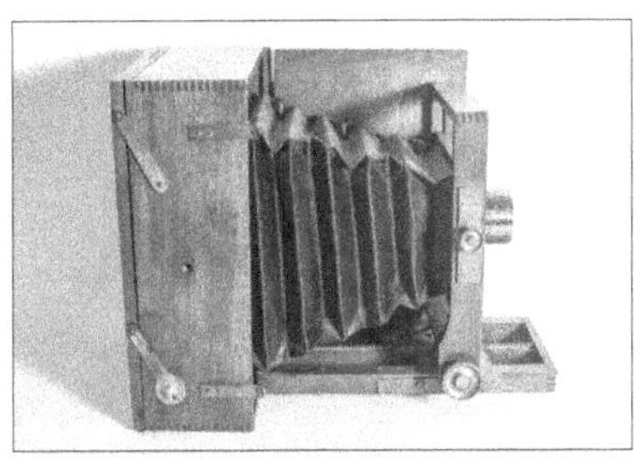

Chapter 20

THE RIDE BACK TO GREENCASTLE is pretty quiet. Nathan and I give each other an occasional glance and smile, but both of us are exhausted from the drama and physical exertion. We finally turn onto County Road 250 North, and Nathan waves at Doc Sanders and his pretty lady friend, Kara, as they stack firewood for the coming winter. It's gratifying seeing normal, wholesome activity after so much turmoil.

A mile later we pull into Nathan's gravel driveway and exit his car. Marla and Clover come out to greet us, and she asks how everything went.

"It's over. I'll tell you all about it later, sweetheart."

The two of them go inside, and Clover and I share some quality time together. We're both enveloped in that special sensation that I always experience here.

"You're happy here aren't you, buddy? I guess we have to make some decisions going forward, huh?" He munches on a dandelion, then hops beside me into the house.

"I don't know about you, Kat, but this old camera collector could use a brief nap. Should we rest up a bit, and then spend some more time in my office?"

"Sounds perfect to me, my friend!"

I lie on the guest bed staring at the ceiling with Clover huddled next to me. There's so much that I need to mentally process that I can't fall asleep. I quickly send my boss, Peaches Panache, a text letting her know that the perpetrator had been caught, and that Detective Shane would fill her in on the details and next steps in the prosecution process. All I want now is some peace in my life.

About an hour later I get up feeling refreshed and walk upstairs to Nathan's office. He's already there sitting quietly looking through one of his antique camera books.

"There you are," he says. "How was your nap?"

"I wasn't able to sleep. I just lied there with Clover, staring at the ceiling, pondering what's next for me."

"Yeah, I wasn't able to sleep either. Marla left a little while ago to run errands, and I decided to come up here to my inner sanctum. So, what have you decided about what you're going to do now? Perhaps, you could manage another office for Wesley Auction House."

"I thought about that, but honestly, I feel like my work here is done. There's something else I yearn to do."

"Oh? Care to share that with me?"

"You're a very special friend, Nathan, and you've been there for this elf maiden like very few mortals ever have, and I'm eternally grateful to you."

"This sounds like the beginning of a goodbye, Kat."

I look at the wonderfully rare cameras in Nathan's office and feel a special kinship with the important collection he's put together, and with him.

"Yes, I believe it is, dear friend, and I think I've found a way to move on in my life ... to finally return home again." I reach over and pick up his Sigriste camera that has brought so many fond memories to me.

"I have a favor to ask of you and Marla."

"Name it, and we'll be happy to do it for you."

"Would you please look after Clover for me when I'm gone? He seems very happy here with you."

"Of course, but I don't fully understand, Kat."

"I know, but please just trust me, as I've trusted you." I clutch the Sigriste camera to my heart, and as I do, Nathan sees a magnificent aura of golden light surround me. The atoms and molecules of my physical being begin to shimmer and dissolve, and I become one with the *lightness of being* ... and then I'm gone.

Nathan rises from his chair with a look of acceptance on his face. He picks up the Sigriste camera and peers into its lens. He'll never forget seeing the scene of Henri and me strolling arm-in-arm somewhere in the south of France. The sun is shining, and he knows that's where I'm meant to be.

I turn, blow Nathan a kiss, and give him one final wave goodbye from across time and space.

THE END

About the Author
Stuart Fabe

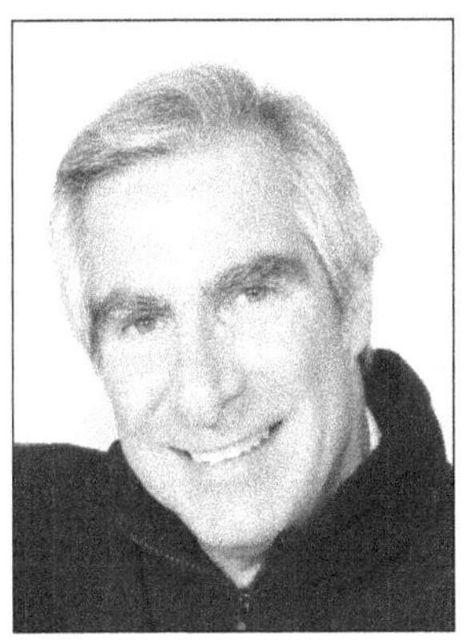

Stu Fabe never thought that he'd ever write a novel, let alone eleven. Throughout his professional career in Cincinnati, Ohio, he worked with troubled youth in the juvenile court system and then switched gears to conduct charitable fundraising campaigns for the Children's Hospital, the Jewish Hospital, and the Cincinnati Zoo.

Raised in an artistic family, Stu said goodbye to Cincinnati and his corporate career at age fifty-five and moved to the countryside just north of

Greencastle, Indiana. There, he and his life partner, Marla, created art and traveled throughout the Midwest exhibiting in art shows for ten years. Then, he settled into photographing the Milky Way and began writing adventure novels.

He's been a country fella for over twenty years now, still writing, still photographing the night sky, while also building one of the finest private antique camera collections in America. It's been the merging of all of these experiences that brought him to write *Moments in Time*.

Chapter Opening Images
Courtesy of Stuartfabecameras.com

Author's Note . . . . American Chamfered Daguerreotype Camera & Original Kodak Camera

Chapter 1 . . . . Polyorama Panoptique

Chapter 2 . . . . Lewis Daguerreotype Camera

Chapter 3 . . . . Camera Obscura

Chapter 4 . . . . Bruns Detective Camera

Chapter 5 . . . . Scenographe Camera

Chapter 6 . . . . French Daguerreotype Camera

Chapter 7 . . . . Billcliff Stereo Camera

Chapter 8 . . . . Jean Sigriste Camera

Chapter 9 . . . . Marion Academy Camera

Chapter 10 . . . . . . Jean Schoenner Magic Lantern

Chapter 11 . . . . . . French Four-Lens Camera

Chapter 12 . . . . . . Gray's Vest Camera

Chapter 13 . . . . . . Pullman Detective Camera

Chapter 14 . . . . . . Adolphe Bertsch Camera

Chapter 15 . . . . . . Photoret Camera

Chapter 16 . . . . . . Kodak Ordinary ABC Cameras

Chapter 17 . . . . . . Luzo Camera

Chapter 18 . . . . . . Scovill Oak Detective Camera

Chapter 19 . . . . . . Lancaster Gem Apparatus

Chapter 20 . . . . . . Lucidograph Camera

* 9 7 9 8 2 3 4 0 4 7 8 5 4 *